THE LAST KNIGHT OF CAMELOT

THE LAST KNIGHT OF CAMELOT

The Chronicles of Sir Kay

Cherith Baldry

To Patsy

Love from
Cherith
x

NEWCON PRESS

NewCon Press
England

First published in the UK by NewCon Press
41 Wheatsheaf Road, Alconbury Weston, Cambs, PE28 4LF
August 2024

NCP339 (limited edition hardback)
NCP340 (softback)

10 9 8 7 6 5 4 3 2 1

Cover art and internal illustration copyright © 2024 by
All stories copyright © by Cherith Baldry

"The King Who is to Come" copyright © 2002, first appeared in *Legends of the Pendragon* (Green Knight Publishing)
"Sir Kay's Ring" copyright © 1997, first appeared in *Sierra Heaven*
"Hunt of the Hart Royal" copyright © 1996, first appeared in *The Chronicles of the Holy Grail* (Raven Books/Robinson Publishing)
"The Avowing of Sir Kay" copyright © 2005, first appeared in *Paradox*
"Sir Kay's Quest" copyright © 1996 (Round Table Publications)
"A Gift for King Arthur" copyright © 1996, first appeared in *Bardic Runes* (Robbins)
"King Arthur's Ransom" copyright © 2001, first appeared in *Scheherazade*
"The Trial of Sir Kay" copyright © 1997, first appeared in *The Chronicles of the Round Table* (Raven Books/Robinson Publishing)
"In the Forest Perilous" copyright © 2000, first appeared in *The Doom of Camelot* (Green Knight Publishing)
"The Last Knight of Camelot" copyright © 1994, first appeared in *The Sharkti Vanguard*

"The Pendragon Banner", "Seeds of Destruction", "The Knight of the Kitchen", "The Flower of Souvenance", and "Sir Kay's Grail" all copyright © 2024, and appear here for the first time.

All rights reserved, including the right to produce this book, or portions thereof, in any form.
No part of this publication may be used to train, inform, or provide source learning data for any chatbot or other form of artificial neural network without the written consent of the copyright holders.

ISBN: 978-1-914953-88-0 (hardback)
978-1-914953-89-7 (softback)

Cover art by Mollyroselee
Cover layout by Ian Whates
Minor editorial meddling and typesetting by Ian Whates

Contents

The King Who is to Come	7
The Pendragon Banner	21
Seeds of Destruction	27
The Knight of the Kitchen	45
Sir Kay's Ring	59
Hunt of the Hart Royal	75
The Avowing of Sir Kay	93
Sir Kay's Quest	111
A Gift for King Arthur	127
King Arthur's Ransom	135
The Trial of Sir Kay	165
The Flower of Souvenance	153
Sir Kay's Grail	181
In the Forest Perilous	187
The Last Knight of Camelot	197
About the Author	201

The King Who is to Come

Kay mounted and trotted briskly down the path from the stable yard. As he came in sight of the practice ground he drew his horse to a halt. A second horseman was riding at the quintain. His lance point struck true in the centre of the shield and the straw figure swivelled round. The rider avoided the swinging sandbag, crouching low over his horse's neck as he galloped away.

Kay sighed, suppressing a moment's envy. The precision, the easy, fluid movement... pure skill. His younger brother, Arthur.

He urged his mount on again, more slowly now, and waited for Arthur, who wheeled his horse at the end of the practice ground and came trotting towards him. He was laughing.

"Where have you been? You said you would ride a course with me."

Kay shook his head. "I can't, not today. I've been talking to Master Benet," he said. "This wet weather makes his joints ache, and he can't ride out to the sheep runs. I said I would go for him. Of course," he added thoughtfully, "he's too old for the steward's job, but Father can't replace him. It would break his heart."

"But you can't go now," Arthur objected. "Surely you haven't forgotten what tomorrow is?"

Once again Kay shook his head. The hard lump of apprehension in his chest, that he had tried for days to ignore, seemed to weigh even heavier. Tomorrow, on the Feast of All Saints, he would be made knight.

"That's tomorrow," he said abruptly. "There's time enough to ride out and talk to the shepherds. The sheep must be down from the high fells before winter sets in."

Arthur grinned and leant over to clap him on the shoulder. "Better today, then. We can't have it said that Sir Kay's first knightly deed was to go and look at sheep!"

"You've been listening to the harpers," Kay said. "But they've turned your head if you think that knighthood is all tournaments and battles with monsters and rescuing fair ladies. It isn't like that here – and not in the rest of Britain either, not since King Uther died. Just one petty war after another until the whole land is sick of it."

His voice began to shake on the last few words, and he stopped himself, appalled, wondering if Arthur had noticed. But his brother gave no sign of it.

"We need a king." Arthur's eyes shone. "A High King, who would set all to rights. We –"

"We're wasting time," Kay interrupted. "And you shouldn't keep your horse standing."

"I'll ride with you, then," Arthur said good-humouredly. He drove his lance point into the ground. "Wait a few minutes while I go and beg some bread and cheese from the kitchen."

Without waiting for Kay's reply, he set off back to the house, his lithe figure straight in the saddle, his tawny hair tossed by the wind. Kay watched him go. Not for the first time, he wondered how it would be to be a knight, and to have a squire who was taller, stronger, more skilled in arms than he was himself. For a moment he imagined the mocking comments of true knights – nobles, kings' sons – if he should meet with them, and he burned with humiliation.

Then he steadied himself, took a breath. His life was not laid out along that road. Besides, if he should ride out on some knightly enterprise, it was impossible to imagine himself with anyone but Arthur at his side.

And that thought led him to what he did not wish to think of. He believed that he could be content, here in this remote valley, with the small duties of the estate that one day would be his own. But Arthur was a younger son, and Sir Ector had no inheritance to give him. When he was made knight in his turn, next Easter or perhaps at Pentecost, Arthur would leave.

He would be the kind of knight the harpers sang of, Kay thought, if anyone could. He would win honour in the tournaments, with a lady's favour fluttering from his helmet, he would come home with tales of battles in distant lands, and all the dragons and ogres he had defeated. If he came home at all.

Kay sighed. He could tell no one – least of all Arthur himself – of the pain that pierced his heart when he thought of the future. Tomorrow, when he became knight, the easy unquestioning world of his childhood would start to crumble.

Impatient with himself, he began to walk his horse slowly away from the practice ground in the direction of the sheep run. He had not reached the edge of the ploughed land before he heard hoofbeats behind him and turned in the saddle to see Arthur. His brother had not only provided himself with a heavy bag of provisions, but a bow and a quiver of arrows slung over his shoulder, and two hunting dogs, his Cabal and Kay's own Luath, loping along beside his horse.

"I thought we might try for a hind," he called out as he came up to Kay. "Something to grace your feast tomorrow night."

Kay shrugged. "As you like."

They set out along the track leading to the fells, with Arthur talking again of his hopes for a king. Kay listened, said little, and tried to hide his impatience.

In this remote valley, battle had swirled around them and gone on. Their father, Sir Ector, had shown no wish to join any of the warring kings. For news they relied on wandering harpers, pedlars, gossip picked up at markets and horse fairs, and the occasional visit from their father's friend, the enigmatic Lord Merlin. Whatever their hopes might be, they had no power to turn them into something real.

"They say that Uriens is a good man," Arthur said. "Would he make a good High King, do you think?"

"Too old," Kay said. "He'd never hold the crown."

"Rience, then?"

"Rience? He's a lout," Kay said disdainfully. "You or I would make a better king."

Arthur laughed. "Rience is trimming a cloak with the beards of defeated kings. I met a horse trader who said he'd seen it with his own eyes!"

Kay made a small, derisive sound. "And did he see if Rience's goats still have their beards?"

Arthur laughed again, and urged his horse into a faster trot. Kay followed, casting an expert eye over the ploughed fields and the grazing land, noticing a thin place in the hedge that would need a stake or two to keep the cattle from straying.

If he had been born a king, he thought, he could have made the whole of Britain into a well-kept estate, orderly and prosperous, instead of draining the land for pointless battles. He smiled wryly to himself. He would wait a long time for a sign that the crown of Britain belonged to him.

They reached the sheep run and the shepherds' hut after an hour's ride. While Kay talked to the shepherds – an old man and a boy, his grandson, who played sharp tunes on a straw pipe – Arthur rode down the hill with the dogs to draw the nearby woods for game.

By the time Kay and the old man had agreed on arrangements for driving the sheep down to their folds, the sun was beginning to go down. There would be little time for hunting, Kay thought, as he said his farewells. Unless Arthur had already killed. Soon they would need to go home, where Kay would prepare to keep vigil in the chapel ready for the ceremonies of the following day.

He rode under the outlying trees, drew rein, and listened. There was the sound of someone crashing through the undergrowth, not far away, and Arthur's voice calling, "Cabal! Cabal!"

"Arthur!" Kay shouted.

He heard the sound of barking, and his own dog, Luath, shot out of a hazel brake and pelted across to stand panting beside his horse. Arthur followed a few moments later. He was dishevelled, and he looked distraught.

"What's the matter?" Kay asked.

"Kay, I've lost Cabal."

"What – how?"

"We started a hind, and chased it, but the trees were too thick, and I couldn't get a shot." Arthur thrust a hand through his hair. "It looked... strange."

"Strange? How?"

"Pale... silvery. Like a Faerie creature. And then it vanished, and Cabal didn't come back when I called him."

Kay's first reaction was that Arthur had lost his wits, but his brother looked so upset that he only said, "The light's going already. Everything looks grey. And Cabal is probably sniffing after rabbits."

Arthur let out a crack of unsteady laughter. "I hope so."

Kay dismounted and led his horse further into the wood. Arthur did the same, and caught up a long branch to poke into the thickets as they passed, all the while calling the dog's name. Luath bounded on ahead.

They followed the tracks back and forth through the forest as the sun sank further towards the west.

"It will be dark before long," Kay said.

"I'm not going home without him!"

Arthur began calling again; just then Kay thought that he heard something else. He put a hand on Arthur's arm. "Wait; listen."

A dog – Luath – barked close by, and then came an answering bark, far in the distance.

"Cabal!" Arthur's face was flooded with relief. "But where is he?"

The barking sounded again. Following the sound, they came to a rocky bank. A spring of water trickled over the stones, and above the place where it spilled out a slab of stone, high as a doorway, was wedged into the hillside. It was rough granite. A ray of the dying sun touched it, and Kay saw markings on it that might have been the carved face of an old man, wreathed with leaves, but so worn away that it was hardly visible.

Luath nosed around it, whining, and from behind it, but still far distant, came the sound of Cabal's barking.

"He's there!" Arthur said. "And listen – there's an echo, as if he's in a cave."

The barking came again, and Kay could hear what his brother meant. For one fanciful moment, he imagined that this might be a hill of the Faerie, and Cabal a prisoner in their enchanted realm. Then he put the thought away, irritated with himself.

"There are caves under these hills," he said. "But how did he get in there?"

Arthur was already scrambling up the bank to examine the stone. Kay followed, until he could see, at the top of the slab, a place where the ground had fallen away. A narrow hole led downwards into night.

"He's down there," Arthur said. "I'm going in after him."

Kay clutched his brother's arm. "Don't be stupid! What if you're trapped down there?" As Arthur pulled obstinately away from him, he added, "You wait here. I'll ride home and bring help – tools, and rope, and something to make a light."

"There isn't time," said Arthur. His face was white and set. "If there are caves down there, he might wander away, and we'd never find him. I'm going after him now. If I can't get out, *then* you can go and get help."

Kay measured glances with him for a moment. He could think of all kinds of arguments, or he could stand on his authority as the elder, so soon to be made knight, but he knew it would be quite useless. Arthur would do what he thought best.

"All right," he said.

Arthur had not waited. He let himself down into the hole and dropped. His tawny hair disappeared in a shower of loose soil, as if the earth had swallowed him. Peering down after him, Kay could see nothing.

"Arthur?" he called.

Silence, for one moment when Kay thought his heart would stop. Then his brother's voice came again.

"Kay – there's a stairway down here!"

"There can't be."

"There is." Arthur's head and shoulders reappeared at the bottom of the hole. His face was streaked with earth and his eyes were alive with excitement. "Come and see. It's quite safe."

Kay felt a pulse of pure terror, even while his mind told him there was no reason for it. The hole was not so deep that it would be impossible to scramble out. And as Arthur withdrew again, Kay could see that there was a tunnel leading off it.

"Wait a minute," he said.

He tethered both horses, spoke a reassuring word to Luath, and then let himself down into the ground, following Arthur.

At first he had to crawl on a floor of loose earth and tree roots, but a few yards further on the tunnel grew suddenly wider, and he could stand upright. A faint light reached down from above, showing him a downward slope, earth giving way to rock cut into shallow stairs. Arthur was standing there, barely restraining his eagerness to go on.

Kay brushed earth from his tunic. "Arthur, this is madness. Without a light…"

"We won't go far," Arthur promised. "Just until I find Cabal. We can come back later with lights."

He led the way down the stairs. Kay followed, glancing back uneasily at the faint spillage of light that showed where the entrance was. Ahead, everything was dark.

He stumbled down the steps, not sure how deeply they were penetrating the hill, until he gradually realised that he could see Arthur as a dark silhouette ahead of him. A silvery light was diffusing upwards from below.

Kay halted. "Arthur!"

His brother turned. His eagerness had become harder, tenser, but Kay could see that he had no intention of turning back. Without speaking, he drew his belt knife and went on.

For a moment, Kay stood still. Down here, with that pale light ahead, thoughts of the Faerie did not seem quite so absurd. Then he realised that Arthur was leaving him behind, and spurred himself into motion again. He hardly knew whether he was afraid to be alone, or wanted to stand beside Arthur to face whatever danger lay ahead.

As he hurried on, Arthur stopped, half turned, and beckoned to him, making a sign for silence. Coming up to him, Kay saw that the stairs had come to an end. Ahead of them was an arched opening. The silvery light poured through it, stronger now, so that at first Kay was half blinded, after the darkness of the tunnel.

Arthur put a hand on his arm, and drew him forward cautiously to the archway. As Kay's vision cleared, he saw that they were standing in the entrance of a vast cave. Pillars of stone soared upwards to a distant roof. The walls curved in an almost perfect circle. No one was there, and there was no sound except for a joyous barking from Cabal, as he launched himself from the other side of the cave and flung himself on Arthur.

While Arthur calmed the excited dog, Kay took a few steps forward. Light diffused throughout the cave, but he could not see where it came from. The air felt cold, moving gently against his face.

In the centre of the cave sat a circular mosaic, a work of the Empire that was gone. It showed two dragons, a red and a white, locked in combat. The white dragon looked larger and stronger, but the red dragon had beaten it down, and one clawed foot crushed its throat. Flames seemed to flicker from its jaws as the glass tesserae caught the light.

In the very centre, with the dragons coiling around it, was a stone table, and on the table a sword. Light glinted from jewels on the scabbard, and smouldered in the rubies that encrusted the hilt. Kay's breath came short, and he raised a hand to his throat, as he felt the power singing out of it.

Around the edges of the mosaic, like petals on a vast flower, were slabs of granite, roughly carved as if they were meant to be couches, with the feet towards the centre. All were empty.

Kay wondered what, or who, would occupy them. He found that he was shivering.

"This is magnificent!" Arthur's voice came from further round the circle. He moved slowly around the outside of the couches, gazing up at the roof of the cave. "What is it? What does it mean?"

"I don't know, and I don't care!" Kay snapped. "Arthur, we shouldn't be here."

"Maybe we should." Arthur paused. "Maybe we would never have found it if we weren't meant to be here."

"Your wits have gone wandering!" All Kay's suppressed fear poured out in irritability. "All this has nothing to do with us – how can it?"

Instead of replying, Arthur plunged forward suddenly, across the dragon mosaic. Kay cried out, half expecting one of the fierce creatures to raise its stone head and blast his brother with fire.

Reaching the table, Arthur leant his hands upon it and gazed down at the sword, his lips parted in wonder.

"Don't touch it!" Kay said hoarsely.

He started towards his brother, wanting to drag him away, but at the edge of the mosaic a chill fell upon him, as if he had been drenched with icy water. While he could still see the sword lying on the table, he felt as if it were raised, flaming, to bar his way. His terror was more for Arthur than for himself, but not even for his brother could he take another step forward.

Arthur laid a hand on the sword hilt, as if he would draw it from the scabbard. Kay tried to shout a warning, but now everything dissolved into a whirling darkness, and he did not know if Arthur could hear him.

The next thing he felt was Arthur's hands firmly gripping his shoulders. The darkness scattered, and he was looking up into his brother's face.

"Kay?" Arthur was frowning, worried. "What's the matter? Are you ill?"

For a moment, Kay leant against him, feeling his warmth and strength, and then, bitterly ashamed, thrust him away.

"Let's go back," he said abruptly. "Bring that damned dog, and let's hope the hole in the hill hasn't closed up."

He expected a protest from Arthur, but his brother scarcely hesitated, only glancing back at the sword on the table. Then he gave Kay a cheerful nod of assent, and whistled up Cabal. This time Kay took the lead, back through the archway and up the stairs towards the world outside.

He had a few bad moments, especially when there was no light ahead to guide them. His heart began to thump uncomfortably, and he was acutely conscious of the weight of earth and rock above their heads. Then he remembered that when they entered the cave the sun had been going down. By now it would be dark outside.

Almost as soon as he recalled this, he came to the head of the stairs and the narrow tunnel, where he had to crawl to reach safety. Then he pulled himself up to the surface again, and crouched for a few moments on the turf, taking in great gasps of the cold night air. The forest surged around him.

The sun had gone, and the moon had not yet risen. The bare branches of the trees were hardly visible against the sky. But the darkness was not unbroken. Kay grew tense again as he saw a spark of firelight a few paces down the hill.

Behind him Cabal scrambled out, scattering earth; he and Luath danced crazily around each other and tore off into the undergrowth. Kay sighed. Little hope now of avoiding notice, if an enemy had made the fire.

Arthur was a dark shape standing over him. Kay rose to his feet and jerked his head towards the firelight. "Visitors?"

"Let's go and see."

Kay drew his belt knife. He gave his brother a fierce look, knowing it was probably lost in the darkness. "*I* will go. Stay back. If there's trouble, ride for help."

No reply, but as Kay picked his way down the slope towards the fire, he could hear Arthur following a pace behind.

Another horse, a magnificent grey stallion, was tethered beside their own mounts. As Kay drew closer, he could see one man alone, bent over the fire, feeding it with branches. He was bundled up in a heavy cloak, the hood pulled down over his face. Something prickled along the length of Kay's spine.

He stepped forward, his knife at the ready, and drew breath for a challenge. It was never spoken.

The man said, "Put that away, Master Kay. You won't need it, unless you care to dress these rabbits for supper."

Well-kept hands rose to put back the hood. Kay found that he was staring at the silver hair and autocratic features of Lord Merlin.

"Merlin!" Arthur's tone was joyful. "What brings you here? Why didn't you ride on to the house?"

"I was waiting for you," Merlin said simply. "Sit down. We may as well share supper. Later the moon will rise, and then we can ride together."

Arthur sat down at once, asking for Merlin's news. For a moment, Kay held back. He had always felt that Merlin took more interest in Arthur than in anyone else in Sir Ector's household – certainly more interest than he took in Kay himself. Kay was not sure he liked it. Merlin, he knew, had been councillor to Uther, the last High King, but there were other stories about him – darker stories of enchantment and shape-shifting and a power that might have come from hell.

In the light of day, Kay did not believe such tales. Here, in a wood at night, with that unearthly cave beneath their feet, he found them more credible.

Beside Merlin were the two rabbits he spoke of, efficiently snared. As Merlin and Arthur talked, Kay skinned and jointed them, balanced them on pointed sticks over the fire and threw the leavings to the dogs. Almost as if he were the squire, he thought ruefully, and Arthur was his knight.

Part of him felt ashamed. Through all that had happened, Arthur had taken the lead, while he had followed, reluctant and afraid. He should not have allowed it. He should have insisted on his own authority, and made Arthur obey him. This was all wrong.

But it had felt right.

When the job was done, Kay went to wash his hands at the spring. As the setting sun had lit the granite slab, now the firelight threw into relief the carving – if it was truly a carving – of the old man's head. Kay studied it, glanced back at Merlin, and his spine pricked again.

As he returned to the fire, he heard Arthur telling Merlin about the cave.

"Such a wonder!" he said eagerly. "Lord Merlin, did you know it was there? Do you know why?"

Merlin bowed his head. "It is for the king who is to come. Long will he reign, and when his reign is over, he will sleep there, with his knights, until the world shall change."

"The king who is to come?" Arthur repeated, as if the rest of what Merlin said had passed him by. "When – now? Is there to be a new king?"

Merlin began to speak of a great tournament to be held in London, at which the High King would be revealed. "I have come to invite your father," he said. "It seems good to me that all three of you should be there."

Arthur laughed delightedly. "Kay, you'll be able to fight in the tournament!"

Kay did not respond. He stood in the shadows at the edge of the circle of firelight. He was barely listening as Arthur went on eagerly questioning Merlin; what could it have to do with them, after all?

Instead he looked at Arthur. He felt a pain he could not describe, to see Arthur: so familiar, so dear to him, and yet suddenly, for some reason, so far away. His brother's face shone in the flames, his amber eyes glowing with excitement; All his being caught up in what Merlin was telling him. The firelight touched his tawny hair and turned it to pure gold, as though he wore a crown.

The Pendragon Banner

The sun was rising. A light wind stirred the heavy folds of the Pendragon banner, and the white hair of the enchanter Merlin, who grasped the stave, on the ramparts of Bedegraine Castle. I felt the power gathering within him, as he watched the two young men who leant over the parapet and gazed down at the wooded slopes below.

"There are eleven kings down there," said Sir Kay, his voice light and edgy. "And their war bands. All of them armed to the teeth and ready to go berserk. We're going to die, Arthur."

King Arthur turned and clapped his foster brother on the shoulder. I saw the sunlight touch his tawny hair to flame, and felt a mute kinship stir within me. "Not today I trust, brother. For Merlin has foretold that I shall be High King."

Sir Kay let out a crack of laughter, and gestured across the battlements to where the besiegers were drawing up their lines. "Perhaps you should tell our guests, Merlin." His laughter died, and he brought his hands down hard on the stone parapet. "The plans we made, Arthur! The dreams we had, the kingdom we meant to build… This stupid waste –"

I had observed these two many times before: the impetuous Kay, hiding fear under a derisive manner; Arthur the king, hiding who knows what under that easy, smiling calm.

"Peace, Kay," he said. "All will be well."

"But they don't listen to you! They don't believe you, or Merlin."

The wizard shrugged. "Belief or not, it was a true foretelling. Fear not to ride into battle, Arthur. There is power on your side that you dream not of. Sir Kay –" He held out the stave. "This banner is yours to bear."

Cherith Baldry

Sir Kay took it from him; a puff of wind rippled over the heavy silk so that the banner stood out stiffly, the golden thread suddenly dazzling in the morning light. Arthur gazed, bright-faced, at the symbol of his kingship.

"Muster the men. We will ride to victory!" he said.

"Indeed." Merlin sighed out the word. The old enchanter drew one finger down the overlapping scales. And I, the dragon on Pendragon's banner, blinked one golden eye and felt the fire grow hot in my belly.

I do not remember the time of my making. They say Merlin wrought me, from fire and gold. Prisoned on the banner, I saw men pass to and fro before me like flickering shadows cast by a lantern. I heard their voices but paid no heed to what they said.

Until he came, the man I learnt to know as Arthur. I was aware of him like the watchfire in a dark forest holding back the night. I saw him and I heard his voice and I knew him for mine. And around him, in his light, I saw the others.

Yet I did not know that I was dragon, or the purpose for which I waited.

The lesser kings who refused to accept Arthur's rule had drawn up their siege lines in the light woodland around Bedegraine. Arthur and his men were trapped inside the fortress. His reinforcements had come up behind the besiegers, but they were too few to encircle them, or to raise the siege. Arthur's only hope was a sortie, to strike through the enemy lines and join the two halves of his force together.

All this I heard in council, where Arthur and Kay and the others wrangled, and Merlin sat silent, with hooded eyes. Even when the horsemen were forming up in the courtyard I did not know what my part was to be. But I saw their brave armour, bright with gold. I

The Last Knight of Camelot

smelt the reek of their bodies and their fear. I knew that I was hungry.

The gates swung open. King Arthur cried, "Forward!" and spurred his horse on, beneath the archway, down the slope towards his enemies. I followed in Sir Kay's grasp, the point of the spearhead of warriors that swept down to destruction. Hoarse shouts and the thudding of hooves were all around me. Sunlight flashed on my scales.

I felt life flow through me. I flexed a claw, stretched cramped muscles, and my forelegs swelled. I clawed at air. Behind me my tail lashed free. I heard the shouting behind me spiral up into terror.

Ground and trees whipped past in the headlong flight of the horses. The banner was puny, a scrap of silk and wood. It could not hold me any longer.

As my wings ripped into the sky, Sir Kay looked up. I saw his face, white with shock and terror. His horse neighed and reared, pawing the air; Sir Kay kept his seat, I grant him that, and his grip on the banner stave, while the rush of Arthur's men swirled round him.

And while the wedge of their attack punched through the line of their enemies and broke into a hundred knots of struggling men, I tore free of my silken prison. I screamed for joy of air and flight and fire. Trees and underbrush leapt into flame, and against that bright background men jerked and panicked and died.

And I, dragon, prisoned no longer, folded my wings and plummeted down upon my prey.

It was soon over. Those who lived fled, while Arthur rallied his own men and sounded the retreat. The slopes below the castle were covered with blackened wood from which smoke still rose in sluggish whorls, and with the bodies of the host that had come against Arthur, invincible in the morning.

I let the updraught from the burning lift me until I grasped the topmost stones of Bedegraine in my talons. And there came Arthur, still bearing sword and shield, his mail clotted with his enemy's blood. Sir Kay was at his shoulder, and the enchanter Merlin at their heels.

Arthur drew in great gulps of air, like a man who has escaped drowning. He threw himself at the battlements, and Kay cried out sharply, as if he thought his foster brother meant to throw himself over.

The king gripped the parapet and looked down to where ravens were gathering over the battlefield. "Merlin – so many dead! Is this what it means to be a king?" Merlin folded his hands into his sleeves and said nothing. "So many good men, who might have followed me if we could have made peace. And now, between sword and dragon fire…"

He turned, and gazed up at me. Bold is the man who looks a dragon in the eye. "And now?" he repeated. "Merlin, what must I do with it now?"

"It is yours," the enchanter replied. "Your birthright as Pendragon. It will serve you."

Sir Kay had folded his arms and leant back against the parapet. "Where will you put it, Arthur?" he asked satirically. "What will it eat?"

"Warriors." The king's voice was sombre.

"Your enemies," said Merlin.

The king still gazed at me; eagles, they say, will gaze straight at the sun. Slowly he shook his head. "The king who rules by dragon power," he said, "will be ruled by it. Dismiss it, Merlin. I will have none of it."

Merlin did not move, or speak. Sir Kay laughed. "Dismiss it? Arthur, look at it! Do you think it will creep quietly back onto the banner?"

The king's mouth was set. "I will not be the dragon king. I want justice, not terror." He spun round to face his foster brother, and gripped him by the shoulders. "Kay, you spoke of the kingdom we will build. But not like this. It will never be what we dreamed of, like this."

Kay flushed, raised his hands to touch his brother's, and said nothing. I am dragon; I stand alone, but what was the pang that went through me then?

The old enchanter looked sour. "I promise you, Arthur, that if you release the dragon now, the day will come when you will wish his power was yours to wield."

"No," Arthur said steadily. "Whatever the cost, Merlin, I will not be such a king."

Merlin faced the king a moment longer, but there was no uncertainty in the look Arthur gave him. Shrugging, he turned to me, his arms raised, ready to speak the word that would banish me. I snapped open my wings; they spanned the top of the tower and shut out the light. I bugled my defiance at the enchanter who had wrought me and imprisoned me. And I saw that he was afraid.

He cried out a word, and pain coursed through my veins. I felt as though chains bound me. I spat flame, and the enchanter gave way before me. The bonds of magic slackened, as if my fire melted them. Merlin cried out again, but his word had lost its power.

He gasped, "Flee! It will destroy us!"

Under the darkness of my wings Sir Kay wrenched free of Arthur's hands and looked up. "Go, worm!" he snapped. "What does a dragon want but gold? You will find more than enough down there – torcs, arm-rings, shield bosses, where British warriors lie dead. And then a hole under the hill, to couch on your hoard and trouble us no longer."

Courageous words, but rash. And neither courage nor temerity will hold back dragon fire. I would have seared him where he stood, if Arthur had not grabbed him and protected both of them under the shelter of his shield.

My flame erupted, but the shield did not burn. I shrieked frustration, as I saw that Arthur had reversed it, and faced me with the inside, where he bore the icon of the Mother of his God.

My fire was ice. Frozen, I gazed down at him, Arthur the king, where he still raised the shield against me, and with his free arm held his brother. He smiled.

"You are magnificent," he said. "But I cannot travel your road. Not in this world, or any other. Go now – but trouble my kingdom again and I will seek you out and destroy you."

I could move again. No man holds a dragon. Not by sorcery, nor by treaty, nor by love. I knew it then, if I had not known it before. I would not think of what might hold me, or what Arthur's words might mean.

I spread my wings, and let the wind take me over the ramparts and into the air above the battlefield. I circled once, and saw the two young men who crouched together, and the wizard alone, their faces upturned to stare at me.

Then the ravens and the scavengers on the ground fled before me as I slid down the sky, down to where gold glinted on the carcasses of the dead.

I am dragon. No wizard's tool, but myself. Glutted, I rest upon a bed of British gold, but the whole world under me is my hoard, and one day I shall rise and claim it.

I will lie here under the hill and sleep. And when Arthur comes again, he will find me waiting.

Seeds of Destruction

"When I look at Mordred and some of the younger men," said Sir Gawain of Orkney, where he sat on a bench at the end of the practice ground, "I start to feel grave and elderly. I think I should hang up my sword and start to be wise."

There was a tiny explosion of laughter from Sir Kay, seated beside him, which was quickly suppressed. "You'll never be grave and elderly," he said.

"Or wise," Sir Gareth added.

"I can still put you on your back, brother, whenever you like," Gawain returned mildly.

Gareth grinned, unrepentant.

"Mordred isn't finding it easy to settle down," Gawain went on more seriously. "If he could forget about Mother, forget about his birth... but I suppose that's asking too much."

"Is it true that Arthur didn't know?" Gareth asked. "About Mother, I mean? Kay, you were there, weren't you? However did it happen?"

All the laughter had died from Kay's face. The hawklike features grew stern and uncompromising. "You don't want to hear about that," he said.

Gawain made himself smile, and laid a hand lightly on Kay's wrist. "There's nothing you can tell us about Mother," he said, "that we don't know already. I'd like to hear how it happened, too."

Kay hesitated, and then nodded reluctantly. "Very well," he said. "It was summer, and the court – if you could call it a court in those days – was at Caerleon. Arthur was seventeen..."

Kay had not thought it possible to be so tired. The meticulous columns of figures on the page in front of him seemed to dance in the wavering lamplight. When he looked up, instead of the flame of the lamp, he saw a bright, fuzzy ball. He blinked away the blur and rubbed the back of his hand across his eyes. He knew he was doing too much of this. The old priest in his father's house was all but blind, from too much poring over ill-written missals. Blind, Kay would be little use to Arthur. He must find someone else, a scribe, or more than one. And where was he supposed to find them, in a country torn by war? Find one, perhaps, and let him teach others.

Kay scribbled a note to himself, put the pen down, and flexed his fingers. For all his weariness, he was satisfied. He had never asked for this job, but he found to his surprise that he was good at it. He could see what needed to be done and how to do it, more easily than many men who were more experienced.

Kay smiled. For all that he was a provincial nobody, catapulted into high position through the accident of being foster-brother to a still more unlikely king, he would build Arthur's kingdom and build it well. Not in its broad outlines and high ideals; it was Arthur who was the kingdom's heart, Arthur who had the gift of lighting a flame in men's minds. But where he led Kay could follow, raising the intricate structure of law and system and ceremony that would give Arthur's ideals body and authority. Kay found that he could dream, and then build the dream in stone and wood and fabric, in words well-chosen and orderly written, in music and light.

He blew out the lamp, groped his way to the door, and let himself into the passage. He moved uncertainly in this still unfamiliar fortress, and then with more confidence as he turned a corner and was guided by the line of light under a door further down.

This room was lit only by firelight. As he stood on the threshold, in that haze of weariness when fanciful thoughts lie very close to the surface, Kay thought the light might almost come from the young man sprawled in a chair by the fire, from tawny hair and compelling amber eyes.

Arthur turned and saw him. "Kay – I thought you'd gone to bed."

"Too much to do."

He went over and curled up on the sheepskins spread before the fire, leaning back against Arthur's chair and reaching up a hand to him. The heat from the fire lapped round him; Kay felt as if he could float in it, like a swimmer in a sunlit sea.

Arthur's voice was warm and amused. "What are you doing down there?"

"In my proper place," Kay replied. "Sitting at your feet. My dear lord," he added, simply for the joy of hearing the words.

In the shock of discovering that Arthur was not his brother, Kay had found happiness in the knowledge that he was his king. When they were boys together, Kay, as the elder – by less than a year – had felt himself pushed into the place of leader. Now he could relax into being what he was always meant to be: Arthur's follower, loving, faithful, safe.

"Don't call me that," Arthur said. "You don't have to. Not when we're alone."

Swiftly Kay turned to look up at him, meeting that warm, lambent gaze. Surely it was not possible, he thought, to go on loving like this. The intensity frightened him. He was not strong enough; something in him would surely break.

"It's what you are," he said. "Lord of my heart, my mind, my life. All that I'll ever be. All I'll ever want."

He had never revealed so much before. Arthur leant towards him; there was love in his face, and wonder and compassion too, and Kay knew, the knowledge piercing like an arrow into his inmost spirit, that his love, this single-minded devotion that could fill his life and be poured out and yet never exhausted, was not returned. Arthur loved him, but not like that.

He could not help shrinking back a little.

"Kay," Arthur said gently.

A hammering on the door interrupted them. Arthur let slip a soft curse, and Kay scrambled to his feet and stood on the opposite side of the fire, his hands clasped behind his back to hide that they were shaking. When the servant entered in response to Arthur's call, he found Sir Kay, High Seneschal of Britain, very stiff, very correct, in conference with his king.

"There's a lady," the servant announced. He sounded put out. "Begging your pardon, my lord. She says she wants to see you."

"A lady? At this time of night?"

"Some problem with her transport, my lord," the man said. "She didn't rightly explain. But she wants to see you."

"Tell her that my lord Arthur has retired for the night," Kay said frostily.

The servant gave him an uneasy look and tugged at the collar of his tunic. "She was... you might say, demanding, sir," he replied.

Arthur sighed and began to get to his feet.

"No!" Kay said. He forced himself to smile, knowing it was a poor effort, trying to pretend that what had just happened had not happened, or that it did not matter. "Let me go. It's my job, Arthur, it's what you keep me for. I'll see her settled for the night, and she can speak to you in the morning." To the servant he went on, "Have rooms made ready for her – the best we can manage – and find out how many of her escort we must lodge."

To his relief, he saw that Arthur was sitting down again. "Very well," the king said. "Go and be diplomatic, you're good at that. But if she's in trouble, or if she's very insistent, let her come. I shan't go to bed yet."

Kay followed the servant down the stairs that led to the main entrance to the castle, as far as a small reception room where the lady waited. When the servant had gone to speak to her escort, Kay braced himself and went in.

The woman in the chair near the hearth could not have shown more disdain if she had been seated in a peasant's turf hut. Kay, bowing formally and striving for an equal hauteur, admitted to himself that she had some cause. The fire had been hastily lit, and still smoked; the walls were bare of hangings; no one had brought refreshment for her. But the fortress was an army headquarters, not a guesthouse for noble visitors.

Kay took a breath and spoke. "My lady, you're very welcome. I am Sir Kay, King Arthur's seneschal. I regret the king has retired for the night."

The lady looked unimpressed. Kay, with a minimal experience of women, supposed that she would be called beautiful, but the beauty was too hard-edged to appeal to him. She was, he guessed, about thirty, with a mass of copper hair piled up in elaborate waves and coils. Her skin was very pale and fine-textured. She wore a green velvet cloak, lined with sables, the gown beneath it silk of a paler green. She was jewelled – gold, and emeralds – befitting a queen.

As Kay's eyes met hers, the cold, green glint like the emeralds she wore, he felt a sudden jolt as if he recognised something in her, as if he had seen, in a momentary flash, the depths of what she was. The sensation was gone almost at once, but it was all he could do not to make the sign of the cross against her.

"Sir Kay," she said, "I will speak with King Arthur."

"I regret, madam, that is not possible. I have ordered rooms to be prepared for you. Go to your rest, and in the morning the king will –"

The hesitation in his speech, which almost disappeared when he was relaxed, was returning to plague him. He needed to take great care in forming his words, almost as if he had been drinking.

The lady interrupted him by rising, a fluid movement that set her silks glittering. "Do you know who I am?"

"No, madam."

"My name is Morgause; I am Queen of Orkney."

Kay felt another jolt of alarm, this time a much more practical one. Morgause's husband, Lot of Orkney, was one of the men who had refused to accept Arthur as king; he had fought against him in the last battle, and even now he was camped out somewhere in the hills, and nobody knew whether he would ask for peace or war. Queen Morgause, Kay realised, could well have walked into Caerleon as a spy.

From the thin smile she was giving him, she had followed his thoughts well enough. "I travel to join my lord," she told him, "taking my sons to their father, and a wheel came off one of my baggage carts a mile down the road. I had expected more hospitality under Arthur's roof, and a more courteous reception."

Kay felt himself flushing. "Madam, I cannot –" he began.

Morgause came close to him; for some reason he was terrified that she would touch him. "My lord has told me of you, Kay," she said. Her tone was barbed, delicate. "A lowborn menial, scarcely fit for knighthood. Don't give yourself a prince's airs. What are you but Arthur's shadow? I've heard tell that you speak with a stammer because your mother took you from her breast to give suck to Arthur. Learn from that how to value yourself, and take me to him."

Kay felt himself giving way before her malice. He took a step back; he could not go on meeting her eyes. Even before he had murmured consent, Morgause had swept past him and stood beside the door, waiting to be conducted to the king.

"But you don't speak with a stammer," Gareth objected.

"Not now," Kay agreed. "But I did, when I was a boy. I never thought about it, until Morgause said… that. Afterwards, I trained myself out of it. It was as if –" He broke off, and sat silent, looking at his hands.

"As if Arthur had wounded you," Gawain suggested. "And instead of letting it heal, you went around displaying it, asking for pity."

Kay flashed him a grateful look. "Yes," he said. "Exactly like that."

"You know," Gawain went on, covering his confusion, "I remember that night. I must have been – what, about thirteen. I remember wondering why Mother ordered the driver to take one of the wheels off the baggage carts. You slept through it all," he reminded Gareth. "We stayed a while in Caerleon, and then left very abruptly. I didn't understand then what it was all about."

Kay's eyes were shadowed. "We know now," he said. "And I let her in. When you tell the story, don't forget that. I didn't know then who or what she was, but I knew she was evil. And I let her in."

With Arthur, Queen Morgause was all graciousness. She explained how her journey had been interrupted by the damaged cart, thanked him for his hospitality, showered him with her good wishes and her hopes for peace. Kay still wondered why she had needed so badly to speak to Arthur that night.

He poured wine for them both, and served it. Morgause took the cup with a glancing flash of venom. He would not be allowed to serve the wine in her household, Kay reflected, much less to be seneschal; he might be lucky to find himself sweeping the floors. Part of him would have liked to withdraw, but Arthur had not dismissed him, and Kay had to admit that he was afraid to leave Morgause alone with the king.

He stood in the shadows, by the table where he had placed the wine jug, listening to Morgause as she spoke, all fire and wit, watching the jewels flash on her long, pale hands, seeing Arthur's smiling response. At last Arthur came across to him, with the wine cups empty. "No, I'll do it," he said, as Kay reached for the jug. "Go to bed, Kay, you're worn out."

Kay was on edge, every nerve end pricking. "It isn't fitting, my lord," he replied, "to leave you without attendance."

Over one shoulder, Arthur cast a laughing look at Morgause. "I think we'll manage," he said.

In that moment, Kay knew, but he remained resolutely obtuse. "I should not wish the Queen of Orkney to think that Arthur is ill-served."

He saw, but pretended not to see, the tiny ripple of impatience that crossed Arthur's face.

"Just go, Kay," the king said.

"Then allow me to conduct the Queen of Orkney to her rooms."

The impatience returned, more clearly now. Arthur gripped his shoulder; he spoke in an urgent undertone. "Kay, take a hint, can't you? You don't need to conduct the Queen of Orkney to her rooms, because she isn't going to go. She's staying here."

It was all Kay could do to keep still, to hold his face expressionless, and pitch his voice at a low murmur that would not reach Morgause. "Arthur, she's the Queen of Orkney. You've been trying to make peace with Lot. Do you think you're going to do it by going to bed with his wife?"

Arthur grinned; there was a wild, reckless look about him. "Lot isn't going to find out, is he? She's not going to tell him."

He turned away from Kay, and poured the wine. He was flushed and excited, his hands not quite steady.

Kay reached out, dared to put a hand on his arm. "Arthur, it's… wrong."

Arthur's grin broadened, and he clapped Kay on the shoulder. "Kay, you should train for the priesthood."

"I didn't mean…"

His voice died as Arthur turned away from him, taking the filled cups across the room and giving one to Morgause. He pledged her, and only then looked back at Kay. He was, suddenly, very much the king.

"Sir Kay, you may leave us. In the morning, please give orders for the repair of my lady's baggage cart."

Kay stiffened, bowed, and went out. In the dark passage, he leant against the wall, shaking with disgust. There was something in Morgause's open triumph, in the speed of her conquest of Arthur, that meant nothing to Kay's intellect, but spoke all too clearly to his nerves and his emotions. But he could do nothing, unless he went back and flung himself at Arthur's feet, begging him to dismiss Morgause. Kay stood for a moment, indecisive, wondering whether to do exactly that. Only the thought of Arthur's reaction stopped him; Morgause's anger, her mockery, he could have lived with.

He went back to his own room, but he could not sleep. He lay through the night, clutching his bed-furs, staring hot-eyed into the dark. His mind was a riot of foul imaginings, his body a single knot of anguish. He could not even weep, or pray.

Even when her cart was repaired, Morgause stayed, as Kay had known she would. He avoided Arthur for four days; it was easy enough to find duties that kept them apart. He could not avoid the gossip; the whole fortress was pulsating with it, but he developed a chilling demeanour that silenced the chattering tongues whenever he appeared.

On the fourth evening his desperate anxiety got the better of him. He intercepted the servant taking a basket of logs to Arthur's quarters, and carried it in himself. Arthur was sitting in the chair by the fireplace, elbows on his knees, his hands hanging loose. He did not look up when Kay came in. Kay knelt on the sheepskins and began, methodically, to set the fire.

After a minute, Arthur said, "Why are you doing that?"

"I wanted to see you."

"And you think you need an excuse? Kay, you're not a servant."

There was a bitter response to that, but Kay stifled it. He sat back and looked up at the king. Instantly, all thoughts of himself were lost in pity. Arthur looked haggard, his face pale, his eyes sunken. The seventeen-year-old boy, warm, vibrant, confident, had vanished utterly.

Hesitantly, Kay reached out and put a hand on his knee. "Arthur, you're ill. Let me call the healers."

Arthur shook his head. "No; tired, maybe. Don't fuss, Kay…"

He glanced, betrayingly, towards the closed door of the bedroom. Kay's fears spilled over. He clutched at Arthur's hands.

"Arthur – please. You must do something. They say she's an enchantress. You must send her away. She'll be –"

He broke off as Arthur rose, thrusting him away so that he fell back against the hearth. "Don't tell me what to do." His voice was grating. "You know nothing – nothing. Get out."

Scrambling to his feet, Kay took one look at Arthur's face, alive with hatred, his humanity almost lost in an animal snarl, and fled.

Kay could have gone to his room to weep away his heartache, but as High Seneschal of Britain he had to take action. He sent for the captain of the guard.

"How many couriers have we able to leave?"

"Tonight, sir?"

Kay stared down his surprise with an icy disdain. "Yes; tonight."

"Four, sir. But it's not –"

"Have them make ready. Send them to me in an hour."

During the hour, he wrote letters. He could not bear the responsibility alone, not any longer. If his father, Sir Ector, whom Arthur still respected as his own father, along with Arthur's chief councillor, the Lord Merlin – if they had been in the court, everything might have been different. Kay would send his couriers to find them; his only regret was that he had not done so days ago.

They came together, many days later, from different directions but within an hour of each other. Kay was summoned to the council chamber to find them there: Merlin, elegant, silver-haired, with an authority and a bearing kings might aim for but seldom achieve, and Sir Ector, heavily suspicious, clothes still stained from travel, but solid as a rock. Kay was thankful just to cross the room and stand beside him.

His father gripped his arm. "Good God, boy, you look terrible. If your health breaks down, what happens to Arthur?"

Kay bowed his head. "I'm sorry."

His father grunted, but the grunt did not sound wholly disapproving. Kay felt a little encouraged, but the feeling vanished as Arthur came into the room and flung himself into the seat on the dais.

"What's this? Am I on trial?" he asked.

Kay could scarcely look at him. The flesh seemed to have shrunk away from his bones. His robe hung on him as if it did not fit any more. His hair was dry, all the light and life gone out of it. His eyes were dull. For the first time, Kay took seriously the rumours that Morgause was an enchantress, that she might have taken Arthur and reamed the heart out of him, and left this husk to take his place as king.

"As we have travelled for some distance, my lord," Merlin said in his beautifully modulated voice, "you might ask us to sit."

Arthur threw out a hand, saying nothing, but they took the gesture for permission. Kay seated himself beside his father, Merlin at a little distance, closer to the king.

"You have the Queen of Orkney under your roof?" Merlin began, a delicate preamble like the advancing of a pawn at chess.

Arthur shot a hostile look at Kay. "And if I have? She was stranded here – was I supposed to lock the gates against her?"

"Better if you had!" Ector said.

Merlin flicked a glance at him, a clear demand for silence. "My lord Arthur," he said. "Let us not waste time. Have you taken this lady to your bed?"

"I thought you knew that."

Merlin's hands closed over the arms of his chair. "Have you?"

"Yes!"

Merlin sat back. Kay thought he looked almost relaxed. When he spoke, his voice was very quiet. "Arthur, you know the Queen of Orkney's parentage?"

The question startled Arthur out of his sullen demeanour, as if it was not what he had expected to hear. "Yes – she's the daughter of Duke Gorlois, and Ygraine."

And your own parentage?"

Arthur stared at him, and then dissolved into unsteady laughter. "Merlin, are you asking me that? When you're the one man who knows all about it? You told me that I'm the son of Uther Pendragon."

Merlin bowed his head. "Yes. And may God forgive me, I did not tell you the name of your mother. She was Ygraine, who wedded Uther after her first husband, Duke Gorlois, was dead." Everyone present anticipated his next words. "Morgause is your half-sister."

Kay felt that his heart had stopped beating. A black chasm gaped in front of him; it would have been the easiest thing he had ever done to let himself fall into it. He felt his father's hand on his shoulder.

"Hold up, boy."

Kay could only cling to self-control by looking at Arthur. The king was unexpectedly calm, frowning slightly as if examining the information Merlin had just given him. Quietly he said, "I did not know." After a moment he added, "Morgause – did she…?"

"Oh, yes, I knew."

The voice came from the doorway. Morgause was standing there; she glittered like a snake with its skin new-shed. "I am with child," she said. "A child that will destroy you, Arthur, and your kingdom." Her smile was openly triumphant, openly contemptuous.

Sir Ector sprang to his feet. "There's one way, madam, that the child need never be born."

Morgause transferred the smile to him, all poisoned sweetness. "You wish it said that Arthur murdered the Queen of Orkney? Along with the other tale – for you might kill me, but a tale is harder to kill. I think not."

Merlin too was on his feet. "You will leave here, madam, you and your escort, within the hour."

She inclined her head to him, and then swept Arthur a deep reverence. "With your leave, my lord. Truly, it is time I went to join my husband. I find the company here… tedious."

She was gone, the silken rustle of her skirts dying away down the passage. When all was quiet again, Arthur said, still in the same flat voice, "I will abdicate, of course."

"You can't do that," Sir Ector protested.

Arthur's head went up, a vestige remaining of his kingliness. "Can't?"

"Men have died to put you on this throne," Sir Ector went on bluntly. "How many more will die if you abdicate? The lesser kings will tear each other to pieces to sit where you sit now."

Merlin was nodding in agreement, before Ector had finished speaking. "Arthur, why do you think I started planning this nearly twenty years ago, when Uther first looked on Ygraine? There is no other successor. No one but you."

Arthur's eyes met his. "And who will follow me now, when they know what I have done? When the child is born? Your shining kingdom, Merlin, has no shining king to lead it. They will cast me out."

Kay knew what he had to do. He could not have spoken, but he needed no words. He knelt before Arthur on the steps of the dais and pressed Arthur's hand to his forehead. It felt very cold.

Almost instantly, Arthur snatched it away from him. He was on his feet, looking down, hard-eyed, at Kay. "No!" His voice was low and charged with fury. "You tried to stop me. You went whining to Merlin… Don't try to pretend now that nothing has changed. Leave me alone!"

He leapt from the dais, pushed past Merlin, and went out.

Ector pulled Kay to his feet. "Get after him, boy. Don't let him go alone. He might do anything…"

Kay did not need telling. He flung himself down the passage, down the stairs, and out into the courtyard, where he caught up with Arthur and grabbed his arm.

"Arthur, don't!" he gasped. "Don't go! Or take me with you. I won't make you angry, I won't even speak, if only you…"

His voice died away at the look Arthur turned on him as he shook himself free. "I told you to leave me alone!"

"I can't – not like this."

He flinched as Arthur caught hold of him, fingers digging painfully into his shoulders. "You'll do as I tell you. If I must be king, I'll be king – I'll be such a king that Merlin would wish he had thrown me over the cliffs at Tintagel instead of bringing me to your father. And I will have obedience!"

Something rose up in Kay, a swelling bitterness that demanded to burst out. "Obedience? Is that all? Your lowest servant gives you that. Is that all you want from me?"

He flung the words at Arthur, meeting the suddenly narrowed eyes.

"I see." Arthur's voice had become quiet, sneering. "You set yourself above obedience. But you know that under any other king you would be nothing, and you're afraid to fall from where I set you."

"You don't know me at all, if you believe that!" Kay retorted.

Arthur released him, thrust him away, almost gently, and took a pace back. All the while his eyes compelled Kay to stillness. He spoke slowly, every word bitten off. "You will leave my service."

The voice was flint, the eyes flint, forcing Kay to his knees. Kay thought that the pain of it would unseat his reason.

"My lord, I cannot live unless I serve you." For a moment Arthur looked down at him, and then without speaking turned to go. "My lord, forgive me!" Kay cried after him.

Arthur frowned, looking back at him, and said harshly, "Forgive you? Who am I to forgive anyone?"

"I shall stay here until you do!"

Arthur started to speak and then broke off. For a few seconds Kay thought that he would reach out a hand to raise him. Instead, he snapped, "Then stay there till you rot!"

Abruptly he strode off across the courtyard, calling for his horse.

"But you can't stop there!" Gareth protested. "What happened after that?"

Kay shrugged; he was looking very tired. "Very little," he replied. "When something is broken, you mend it and go on as best you can."

"And if it can't be mended?" Gawain asked quietly.

Kay was looking at his hands again, playing with his ring, the carnelian set in gold that the king had given him.

"Truly," he said, "I think something was broken in me that day. When the solid earth beneath you gives way, and you find yourself struggling in a swamp… It made me mistrustful, I think, and less gracious than I might have been." He looked sideways at Gareth, and a gleam of wry humour surfaced out of his heartache. "Downright rude, you would say, Sir Gareth?"

Gareth gave him a luminous smile. "Dear Kay, don't ever change," he said. "How would we recognise you? But finish the story," he added. "How long did Arthur keep you in the courtyard?"

Kay's mouth twisted. "Longer than I bargained for…"

Kay's eyes were fixed on his father's feet, planted uncompromisingly on the stones of the courtyard in front of him. Scarred riding boots, the creases still engrained with the dust of the road.

"Look at me, boy," his father barked.

Obediently Kay raised his head. Sir Ector was white, on the verge of one of those rages that had terrified Kay when he was a boy.

"What in heaven's name do you think you're doing?" he demanded.

"I... angered the king," Kay explained. "I said that I would stay here until he forgives me."

His father snorted. "While he's gone riding off as if all the legions of hell were at his heels. I told you to stay with him."

"He wouldn't have me."

"And how long do you intend keeping on with this... ludicrous demonstration?"

Kay set his mouth to stop it from trembling, knowing his father would see only obstinacy. "As long as I must."

Sir Ector glared at him. "Does this vow of yours stop you from eating, if I bring you something out here?"

"Yes, it does," Kay snapped, the unexpected kindness almost breaking his resolve.

His father strode off without another word. A few minutes later he was back, slamming a jug of water down on the stones beside Kay so hard that Kay half-expected it to shatter, and putting Kay's cloak around his shoulders. Briefly Kay felt his father's hand grip hard on his shoulder, and looked up in surprise, to see no more than Sir Ector's retreating back.

Kay stayed where he was, his eyes cast down. He could hear movement and voices around him, even some laughter, though that was uneasy and quickly broken off. For a short time he was worried that Morgause, as she left, might pass and find him here, but he knew she would use the main gate, not this postern, and as time went by he realised that she must have gone. Gradually the daylight failed.

It was full dark when Arthur came back. Kay recognised his footstep, but he did not look up until the king stood in front of him. For a few seconds he caught on Arthur's face an open, shocked expression.

Arthur said, "Kay…"

Kay gazed up at him, mutely pleading. He saw Arthur's face grow hard again, and he turned away. Kay watched him go, and then drew his cloak around him to face the night.

In the end Kay was never sure how long he spent in the courtyard. The next day was clear enough, punctuated only by another harangue from his father. He was growing light-headed with fatigue, his body a long, nagging ache. In the evening, heavy rain set in; the sodden folds of his cloak clung to him, and he began to shiver. His head was burning.

At some time during the following night, his grip on time and reality failed him. He must have slept, or lost consciousness; he woke while it was still dark, and found himself in an untidy huddle on the stones. Painfully he pushed himself back on to his knees, groped for the water jug and realised that at some point he had knocked it over. A whimper of sheer desolation escaped him, and he clenched his teeth on what could become an animal howling.

His head swam; without being conscious of movement, or time passing, he realised that he was sprawling on his back. Stars blazed down on him, burning out his sight. Very slowly, every movement a tearing agony, he dragged himself across the courtyard until he could support himself against the stable wall. He wondered vaguely if that was to break his vow.

There was no dawn the next day, only a grey twilight, in which blurred shapes swelled and shimmered; he had pored too long over his accounts, and his sight had failed him. Sound echoed around him, while deep inside his brain a grindstone turned rhythmically.

Then he was looking down on himself, very small and distant, but very clear. His father was there, too, and servants, but he could not see Arthur. They had stripped the body, and were bathing it. Kay heard his father's voice, very close, and sharp. "Hold his head up, fool!"

They were trickling something into his mouth, something warm and sweet, with a bitter aftertaste. And after that, nothing but a long, soft darkness.

Kay opened his eyes on a room lit only by firelight. Fur brushed his cheek. He lay in bed; gradually he recognised his own room. He felt utterly empty. He had broken his vow. There was no hope left, not anywhere in the world.

"Kay?" It was Arthur's voice, close by. "Kay, are you awake?"

Kay turned his head. Arthur crouched beside the bed, bending over him. He was, once more, recognisably Arthur, but somehow older, harder; the eager, confident boy had gone far beyond Kay's power to call him back. Kay knew he had failed. He would have laid down his life for Arthur, but Arthur had not needed it. He had needed someone older, more experienced, more sure of himself, or perhaps, simply, someone who had known the truth.

"I broke my vow," he said.

He felt Arthur's hand close round his. "No," the king said. "I forgave you long ago – or saw that there was nothing to forgive. But I was too proud and stubborn to tell you. I'm sorry, Kay. I almost lost you."

He moved out of the range of Kay's vision, and came back with a cup in his hand. "Merlin said you should have this when you woke."

Kay remembered the drug and turned his head away. "No."

"Come on – it's only milk and spices."

Gently he raised Kay's head and held the cup for him. Kay swallowed a little of the milk, but its taste was cloying, and he wanted to be sick. Arthur let him lie back again.

"Your father was furious with me," he said. "He wanted Merlin to go and talk to you." Faintly, he smiled. "Merlin said that as you were the only person in the whole place who was displaying even a scrap of common sense, why should he try to stop you?"

Kay was vaguely surprised. He had never expected to win Merlin's approval. He and Arthur might have laughed together over that, once. He made himself listen to what Arthur was telling him.

"I've been the sort of king I could be – just for a few days. Wild, tyrannical, caring for nothing but my own passions. The sort of king

I must never be again. It was the thought of you that pulled me up, in the end. Not soon enough. Kay." When Kay said nothing, he went on, "I could give you lands of your own, if you would like that."

Kay stared at him for a minute, the fire warm on tawny hair, the play of light and strong shadow. He tried to speak, but he found it difficult once more to form the words. "You want… to send me away?" he said at last.

"No!" Arthur's hand grasped Kay's again. "Only if you want it."

Kay knew that before all this, before Morgause, Arthur would never have asked that question. They had both accepted, without even thinking about it, that Kay's place was at Arthur's side. Kay wanted to weep, but all his tears were dried up.

Arthur said, "I know you don't want power for its own sake. I should never have said that to you. But I couldn't believe, after what I did, that anyone would want to serve me for myself – even you, Kay."

He looked down at Kay's hand, held between his own, and touched the ring, his gift, which Kay still wore. Kay wanted to cry out love from his shattered heart, but the memory of failure closed his throat. At last he managed to say, stumbling again over the words, "I shall never… *never* want anything, except to serve you."

He saw Arthur's smile break through, like the sun through cloud, strong, warm, as if at last hope might revive. To Kay, it was infinitely distant. He did not know, any longer, how to respond to it. He closed his eyes, and hoped that Arthur would think he slept.

As Kay brought the story to an end, Gareth had drawn closer to him, and put an arm round his shoulders.

"Somehow, after that, I never really liked Caerleon," Kay said distantly.

"Don't grieve," Gareth murmured. "It's over."

Gawain sighed faintly. "Oh, no," he said. "It's never over."

He was gazing out across the practice ground, where his half-brother Mordred had just drawn his sword.

The Knight of the Kitchen

Gareth of Orkney balanced the tray carefully in one hand, and knocked on the door with the other. Not waiting for permission, he opened the door and went in.

Sir Kay was sitting at his huge work table, a pen in his hand. He looked up irritably. "What is it, boy?"

Gareth relaxed slightly. When he came to court he had not told his name, and his brothers, who knew it anyway, were sworn to silence. If Sir Kay was in a relatively good mood, he called him 'boy', or 'lad'; if he was in a bad mood he had a selection of maliciously imaginative nicknames, some of which were apt enough to draw blood.

"You haven't eaten anything today, sir," Gareth replied.

He held out the tray; it bore a jug of wine, bread, and fruit which Gareth suspected had been meant for the great feast tonight. "The bread's fresh, sir, just out of the oven," he said. "It's still warm."

Kay sighed wearily and waved a hand towards a smaller table in the window alcove. "Put it over there."

Gareth obeyed, steering round Luath, the old hunting dog, who lay somnolent in a patch of sunshine; he raised a grey muzzle and looked at Gareth incuriously. Gareth poured the wine, and wished he dared bully Kay into having his breakfast.

"You haven't gone to the tournament," Kay said.

"You haven't given me leave, sir."

"Leave?" Kay made an impatient gesture. "You can have leave, if you want it. You should have asked. Here."

He poked among the litter on the table, found a coin, and tossed it towards Gareth, who snapped it out of the air like a swift taking a fly.

"Thank you, sir."

"You can go now – take a horse from the stables. You won't have missed anything. There are always interminable ceremonies before they get down to the serious business of breaking each other's necks."

Gareth grinned. "Thank you!"

At the door, he hesitated. Kay had picked up his pen and started to write again. Gareth studied the dark head. Dressed for a day's work, Sir Kay was unostentatious – the threadbare tunic, the shirt under it clean but mended. Gareth had just been watching the other knights leave in all their magnificence, bright colours and brighter steel. He searched for words.

Not looking at him, Kay asked, "What are you hovering about for?"

"I – I'm sorry, sir, but..." He still hesitated. Oh, God, he thought, why can't I just go, instead of standing here about to make a fool of myself? Desperately he launched into his question. "Sir, don't you want to go?"

Kay's dark eyes were snapping at him. Inwardly, Gareth flinched.

"What I may or may not want is immaterial," Kay said incisively, "when there is a feast tonight which needs preparing, and the best part of the court out at the tournament field. Besides, I've always considered that being battered to a pulp is one of the less desirable forms of entertainment. Get out."

Gareth muttered acknowledgement, and went.

On his way to the stables, Gareth had to pass by the guesthouse. He had been there on the previous evening, helping to unload the packs of a group of merchants who had arrived too late to display their wares. Now he slowed his pace, wondering what the merchants were doing and whether, with all the other things he had to organise, Kay would have time to see them.

From one of the windows came a hard, clattering sound; Gareth actually went on a few more steps before his mind caught up with what his ears had heard. The sound of a sword being dropped on to a stone-flagged floor. Softly, Gareth retraced his steps, flattened himself against the wall outside the window, and warily peered inside.

The merchants were arming. Their packs spilled weapons. They moved swiftly, in silence. Almost before he had taken in what he had seen, Gareth was speeding back the way he had come. He flung open the door of the workroom; Kay winced as it crashed back against the wall.

"What do you –" he began, and broke off as Gareth began to gasp out his story.

By the time he had finished, Kay had come to his feet and was standing in the doorway, looking down the stairs into the passage below.

"What are we going to do?" Gareth asked.

Kay beckoned him forward, signing him to silence. The old hunting dog heaved himself to his feet and made to follow. "No, Luath; stay," Kay said, and closed the door.

With Gareth behind him, he began to move cautiously down the stairs. "We'll try to lock them in the guesthouse," he said, touching the bunch of keys at his belt. "That will hold them for a while. And then you can take a horse and ride to warn the king."

"But who are they?" Gareth asked. "And why do they –?"

Kay's mouth tightened. "Do you think Arthur has no enemies? Take the castle when it's almost empty, with their main force waiting to trap Arthur from behind? If I had to guess, I would say King Mark of Cornwall. It has his treacherous stamp."

He came to the bottom of the steps and paused. Everything was still quiet. He laid a hand lightly on Gareth's arm. "Go into the kitchen," he said, "and bring two knives. Don't say anything to alarm anyone."

"I won't," Gareth assured him. "There's no one left there who can help, anyway. They're none of them trained to fight."

Kay cocked an eyebrow at him. "And you are?"

"Yes, I –" Gareth broke off. That was part of his past that no one was supposed to know about. He shrugged. "In a way," he said.

To avoid any more questions, he sped off towards the kitchens. No one was there except for the cook and her maids busy with the preparations for the evening's feast, and none of them paid Gareth any attention. He took two long knives, almost the size of short swords, and returned to Kay.

Kay reached out, took one of the knives, and padded on quietly down the passage, towards the door that led to the courtyard. "If there's trouble," he said, "you don't try to be a hero. Take a horse and you get out. Is that understood?"

Gareth hesitated; Kay stopped and faced him, with the imperious look that had quelled whole tribes of kitchen boys. "Is that understood?"

"Yes, sir."

Satisfied, Kay moved on, and edged the door open. Then he stiffened. Looking over his shoulder, Gareth could see across the courtyard to the main gate. It was open and armed men were slipping quietly through. Close by was a sprawl of bodies, grimly motionless.

"Too late," Kay breathed. "Get back."

But as he closed the door there came a shout from across the courtyard, and the sound of pounding feet approaching the door. Kay struggled briefly to turn the key, but the lock was stiff, and there was no time. He gave up, thrusting Gareth back along the passage.

"Go through the workroom," he ordered, pushing the keys into Gareth's hands, "down the back stairs and try the postern gate. You might get through. I'll hold them here."

The door crashed open. Feet thudded down the passage. "No," Gareth said.

Kay turned a look of fury on him, but there was no time to argue. Their attackers were on them.

Gareth had never before faced someone who was trying to kill him. Part of his mind remained quite cool, counting their enemies – too many – remembering to allow for the shorter reach of his weapon, and thankful for the armsmaster at home who had drilled him so that everything he must do had become automatic. Another part of him watched the dancing blades with a sick terror. And he could still reflect that afterwards, if they survived, Kay was going to take him to task for disobeying a direct order. It might be easier to get killed now and have done with it.

Beside him, Kay fought with clean, economical strokes, more for defence than attack, allowing himself, with Gareth, to be forced back up the stairs towards the workroom. Gareth thought he could divine his plan; if they could reach the workroom, and lock the door on their attackers, they might still escape, together, through the postern.

Until they reached the landing, it seemed as if they had a chance. But once they were off the staircase there was more space for their attackers to surround them. Gareth broke away, and thrust the door open; in those few seconds, the invaders closed round Kay. He shouted at Gareth, "Go!" but Gareth flung himself back into the fight, feeling a fierce satisfaction as his knife slid home, and one of the men fell writhing to the floor.

Kay fought like a demon; already two others had fallen, but he could not guard his back, and one of the men leapt on him from behind, bearing his sword arm down, leaving him defenceless. Gareth, locked into combat with another of them, could not reach him. Then from the open door the old dog, Luath, launched himself, snarling. Dog and man rolled over and over in the doorway. Gareth tripped, and dragged his adversary down with him.

He was on top of his attacker, his knife raised, when someone grabbed him from behind and hauled him to his feet. However frantically he struggled, he could not break free. Panting, he stood on the threshold of the workroom, pinned back against the wall by an invader on either side of him.

On the opposite side of the door, Kay was pinioned too. The right sleeve of his shirt was slashed into ribbons, and blood oozed from a long gash down his forearm. He looked furious.

The leader of the attackers went over to him and laid the point of his sword in the hollow of Kay's throat. Gareth got a good look at him for the first time. He was tall, with straggling grey hair and a sneering expression. No knight, Gareth could see, but a footsoldier, perhaps a paid mercenary.

"Now," he said to Kay. "To start with, tell us who you are."

Kay straightened, his head flung back. "I am Sir Kay, King Arthur's High Seneschal."

The warrior grinned. "Oh – Sir Kay." The repetition of the name was an insult. "We've heard about you, haven't we, lads? And this?" he added, jerking his head towards Gareth.

"A kitchen boy," Kay said. "Unimportant. You can let him go."

"A kitchen boy who's a bit too handy with a knife," the warrior said. "We'll hold on to him for the time being. Now – you." He jerked the sword and a bead of blood welled up at the point. "Tell me – when does Arthur come back from the tournament?"

"This evening," Kay replied cautiously.

"And before that? Is he expecting any word from you before then?"

For the first time Kay seemed uncertain. He moistened his lips; his eyes shifted uneasily, looking everywhere but at his adversary. Something cold stabbed in the pit of Gareth's stomach.

"Well?" the warrior asked.

The sword bit deeper and Kay shrank back against the doorpost. His fear was obvious now. "Don't," he said. "Don't, you're hurting me. I'll tell you."

"No!" Gareth burst out.

Kay did not even look at him. He was speaking again, gasping out the words, eager to win his safety from that sword point. The cold sensation spread over Gareth. He had heard the sniggered remarks about Kay; everyone said that he was a coward. Gareth had hoped that it was not true. Kay had fought with splendid courage on the stairs, so what was the matter with him now? Gareth tried to understand, tried to imagine how he would feel if he was seconds away from having his throat cut.

Kay was helpless; he was a small man, spare and lightweight, his fighting skills depending on intelligence rather than physical strength, and either of the men who held him could have broken him apart with their bare hands, even if their leader had not held the sword. Kay had no choice but to speak or die. And Gareth very much did not want him dead. He could not understand why he was feeling so sick.

"There are carts – two carts," Kay was saying. "They're to go up to the tournament field with food for the mid-day meal. They should be ready by now, loaded in the courtyard. If you send them in the next hour, Arthur won't know that anything is wrong."

The warrior stood looking at him, obviously having it in mind to kill him anyway.

"No – no, don't!" Kay gasped, trying to press himself back against the door.

The warrior grunted and lowered the sword. "You might be useful again," he admitted. "For the time being, you can stay here."

He turned to Gareth and wrenched the bunch of keys out of his belt, crossed the workroom and locked the far door. Gareth had been hoping that he would have overlooked it. At a sign from him, his men thrust Kay and Gareth inside, and the main door too was locked against them. Gareth heard footsteps clattering off down the stairs.

He stood looking at his feet, not at Kay, because he thought that his disappointment must be showing in his face, and he was too embarrassed to let Kay see it. He was still trying to think what to do or say next, when he heard Kay's voice, strained almost to breaking.

"Luath."

Near the door, the old dog lay on his side, his limbs twitching. Blood was pooling on the floor. As Kay knelt down and took the head on to his lap, the dog gave one final spasm, and was still. Kay crouched over the body.

"He died trying to protect you," Gareth said.

"We used to hunt with him," Kay said, still in the same tight voice. "Arthur and I, when we were boys together. He was the finest –"

He broke off. Gareth stared at him, horror-stricken. Kay, weeping? *Kay*, who was widely reputed to have a chunk of ice where his heart should be? Gareth took a step towards him; stopped; did not know what to do.

At last he said, knowing his voice was unsteady, "They've hurt your arm. Let me see to it."

He poured wine into the wound, and bound it up with strips torn from the cloth on the breakfast tray, contriving a sling out of the napkin. Kay remained still, unresponsive, neither helping nor hindering him.

Only, as Gareth was tying the bandages, he said unevenly, "You realise that I'll have to rewrite the linen inventory?"

The wretched attempt at a joke tightened Gareth's throat and left him helpless. He wanted to comfort Kay, and he did not dare. He was making the final knot in the sling before he could speak again. "Does that feel better, sir?"

"No, it does not feel better." Kay was snarling again; irrationally, Gareth was heartened. "It hurts like hell. But I'm not one of your sniffling kitchen-maids, needing to be fussed over. Bring me some water." Gareth poured a cup from the jug on the work table and brought it to him. Kay drank and then got up, laying Luath's head gently on the floor again.

"Now," he said, "it's time we were moving."

"But how can we?" Gareth asked. "We're locked in; they took the keys."

Kay stared at him, a look that he might have given to a pile of floor sweepings. "I was right, they must be King Mark's men," he said. "Not only treacherous, but stupid as well."

The Last Knight of Camelot

He crossed the room, flung open a chest, scrabbled around in it for a moment, and straightened up with another bunch of keys in his hand. Gareth laughed.

"Don't look so surprised," Kay snapped. "Now, listen –"

Instead of listening, Gareth interrupted. "We need to get a message to the king. If the carts didn't go, then –"

He broke off. The intent look Kay was giving him told him, too late, that he should have kept quiet.

"So that's it," Kay said softly. He was white, dishevelled, in pain, but he was standing very straight, with arrogance in every line of his hawk's face. "You think Kay went to pieces, don't you? Oh, I know what they say about me! You think I would serve the king better with my throat slit?"

That was so close to what Gareth had been thinking that he could find no answer. He flushed and said nothing.

Kay flung away from him across the room; jerkily, he said, "Start thinking with your head, boy, instead of your guts. If the carts don't go, what happens?"

"I don't –"

"I'll tell you. Arthur sends a messenger, to find out what went wrong. And Mark's men know that Arthur is warned. They bolt the gates and set archers on the walls and settle down for a good long siege. Whereas if they think Arthur and his knights are happily occupied, pretending to kill each other, they might get a little careless."

Gareth knew he was grinning stupidly; he did not care. "Tell me what you want me to do."

Sir Kay stood, alert, in the kitchen store room which looked out over the main courtyard. He was not alone. At the windows, three bowmen were crouching. Sir Marhaus, brought from the castle infirmary where he was recovering from a fever, and grumbling that the bow was not his weapon. Sir Gaheris, who had broken an ankle in a fall from his horse, but who had managed to get himself across to the kitchens with a crutch and an inexhaustible fund of curses. And Sir Ulfin, too old to have much interest in the tournament, but not so old or so dim-sighted that he could not put an arrow through the throat of an invader.

Their main force, Kay thought, was still close to the courtyard and the gates. His cautious movements around the castle had not been observed. Though the invaders had thought to put a guard on the armoury, they had forgotten the workshops, or perhaps they had not had enough men; there he had found the bows and arrows, and although with his arm injured he could not manage a bow, he had provided himself with a sword.

He realised that he was clenching the hilt too tightly, and made himself relax. Marhaus, waiting, muttered, "I hope the lad got through."

Silently, Kay echoed his hope. Sending the boy up to the tournament field hidden in one of the carts had been an obvious move; he did not like to think of what might have gone wrong.

"He'll get through," Gaheris said, sounding oddly confident. "He knows what he's about."

A sudden movement in the courtyard below. Kay gripped his sword. There was the sound of distant shouting, and more of the invaders appeared. Slowly the gates began to swing open.

The carts had returned, this time laden with knights already wounded in the tournament. There seemed to be a large number of them. Kay hoped that Arthur had not overdone it, and aroused the invaders' suspicions, but as he had hoped the taking of hostages – wounded hostages – proved too much of a temptation. The carts were allowed to enter.

Looking over Gaheris' shoulder, Kay could make out individuals among the bodies sprawled in the carts. Lancelot. Bedivere, looking thoroughly dead. Griflet. Gaheris' brother Gawain, hanging out of the back of the second cart with his honey-gold hair sweeping the dust of the courtyard. The drivers of the carts were heavily cloaked, to hide the fact that they were not the same drivers who had left.

Kay felt as though something were stopping his breath. The gates were closing, the carts lumbering to a stop. Sir Ulfin gave a keen sound of satisfaction as he fitted an arrow to his bow.

Not yet, Kay thought, and then, *Now!*

A shout split the silence. Arthur's knights sprang up, came boiling out of the carts, their weapons raised against the astonished invaders. In the store room, the bows sang. Caught between two attacks, the invaders began to panic. Kay allowed himself one look before hurrying down to join the fight; in that look he saw one of the drivers throw off his cloak, recognised the height and the bright chestnut hair… his kitchen boy, who should have been safely at the field! Kay wrenched the door open and ran down the stairs.

By the time he reached the courtyard, most of the fighting was over. A few of the invaders lay dead or wounded; the rest were prisoners. One or two skirmishes were still going on, but as Kay took in the scene the remaining fighters realised they were hopelessly outnumbered, and threw down their swords.

His kitchen boy broke away and came over to him, his face vivid with excitement. "It worked!" His voice was exultant. "Sir, it was marvellous! It worked like a dream!"

Agravaine, passing by, clapped him on the shoulder. "Well fought, lad." His glance went past the boy and fell on Kay, who drew himself up to meet the contempt in his face. "I might have known," Agravaine said, "that you would appear when it's all over."

He went on. The boy looked after him, beginning to say, "But it wasn't —" and breaking off as he realised that Agravaine was not attending to him. He turned back to Kay. "Sir, I'm sorry. They all think it's something I did. I keep trying to tell them, but they won't listen."

If he had shown pride in himself, Kay could have borne it, but he was scalded by the boy's distress. "What are you doing here?" he asked abrasively. "You should have stayed at the field, out of the way, and left this to the experienced fighters."

He had expected his words to crush the boy, but he showed no sign of being crushed. "The king gave me leave, sir," he replied politely.

"And there's the matter of the order I gave you."

The boy blinked at him in puzzled innocence. "Order, sir?"

"You disobeyed a direct order."

The boy's gaze was fixed blandly on a spot over Kay's shoulder. A muscle was twitching at the corner of his mouth. "I must have misheard you, sir."

Kay felt himself beginning to shake. He could have thought of a punishment that would have kept the boy slaving for the next fortnight. Or he could have put his arms round him and thanked God for his safety. He did not know himself which he wanted to do. Instead, he swung round and stalked off down the passage.

Gareth did not want to hear anyone else singing his praises. The day had grown curiously flat. He went back to the kitchens, where he managed to break a bowl, and got under everyone's feet until the cook gave him some herbs to chop for the evening meal.

He was still at work when he felt a touch on his shoulder. Kay stood behind him; he looked white and strained. "Leave that," he said. "Wash your hands and come up to the workroom."

When Gareth arrived, Kay was bending over the body of Luath, wrapped now in a white linen cloth.

He looked up. "I want you to –" He broke off. He was finding it difficult to ask what Gareth already guessed he wanted. At last he said abruptly, "I can't manage alone, not with this arm. Will you come with me and help me to bury him?"

They rode a little way out of the city, to where alder trees leant over a small stream. While Gareth dug the grave, Kay sat on a rock, with Luath's head in his lap. He had folded back the linen wrapping, and was stroking the short, silky hair on the muzzle and round the ears. He said nothing; Gareth thought that he was crying, but he went on digging and resolutely failed to notice.

When Gareth was ready, he helped Kay to lower the body into the grave. Kay stooped over it for a moment longer, and then rose and stood with his back turned.

Gareth began to fill in the grave. He suggested, "We could plant something here – sage, or rosemary, if you like. We could bring it up tomorrow."

Daylight was fading to dusk, and there was no sound except for the murmuring of the stream. Gareth had time to wonder whether he had said something immeasurably stupid, before Kay uttered one word, a choked out, "Yes."

It was dark by the time they returned to the castle. In the courtyard Gareth dismounted and walked round the horse to help Kay. "You look awful, sir," he said frankly. "You should go to bed."

Kay swung himself to the ground, awkwardly, but ignoring Gareth's outstretched hand. "Arthur holds his great feast tonight," he said. "Or have you forgotten? We both have work to do. Take the horses back to the stable, and then go and get on. And scrub out those filthy fingernails before you go anywhere near the kitchens!"

Kay somehow found time to bathe, change and have his arm properly dressed before the feast was due to begin. Returning along the passage from the kitchens to the great hail, he encountered his kitchen boy again. The lad had trapped Gawain of Orkney against a pillar, and he was explaining something with a great many excited gestures. Kay drew near enough to listen.

"And you should have seen Kay!" the boy was saying. "With no more than a kitchen knife, and –"

"Boy!" Kay's interruption sounded harsh even to his own ears.

The boy swung round to face him. "Oh, sir, I was telling Gawain how –"

"*Sir* Gawain has doubtless better things to do than listen to the vapourings of a kitchen boy. And there's still work to be done. There'll be time enough later to tell about all your glorious deeds."

"But it was you I –" The boy began to protest, and then suddenly his indignation dissolved into affectionate laughter. Kay felt seared by it. "Very well, sir," the boy said. "At once, sir."

He bowed and sped off.

"Incorrigible," Gawain murmured.

"He would make a fine knight," Kay said absently, scarcely aware that he was speaking his thoughts aloud.

"He will, one day," Gawain replied.

Kay turned to him, braced for a rebuke, but though Gawain looked amused, there was no mockery in his face. He indicated the stairs that led to the great hall. "Shall we go?"

Kay took a step backwards, glancing towards the kitchens. "I – I have duties."

Gawain – golden, languid, smiling – came to him and took him firmly by his uninjured arm. "Rubbish! If you don't sit down, you're going to fall down. Anything you have to do will get done without you, or you haven't frightened them properly. You're going to come with me and tell me all about it."

It seemed impossible to refuse. Kay felt too exhausted to go on arguing. And, he thought confusedly, Gawain had always been kind. He would have preferred to face another company of armed invaders, but instead he let Gawain draw him up the stairway towards the music and laughter of the great hall. He did not notice Gareth reappearing behind them, carefully balancing a covered dish, or his kitchen boy's nod of satisfaction at seeing them together.

Sir Kay's Ring

Gareth of Orkney set the log basket down in the hearth and began, carefully, to build up the fire. The room was a small one, in the king's private suite. Behind Gareth, the king was seated at a table with Sir Kay, Sir Lancelot, and Sir Gawain, Gareth's elder brother. They were discussing the visit of the ambassador from Cornwall.

During the time that he had been working in the kitchens at Camelot, Gareth had learnt many things; one of the most useful was that if you kept quiet, and found a job to do, hardly anybody noticed you or told you to go away.

"I've met this ambassador, this Sir Andret, before," Lancelot was saying. "I don't like him and I don't trust him."

"No," the king agreed. "He says he seeks for peace. But he has been here a week now, and all I have from him is flowery compliments." An audible sound of contempt, which Gareth guessed came from Sir Kay, punctuated the king's words. "Either Sir Andret is a spy," Arthur went on, his measured voice undisturbed by the interruption, "or he delays us while his lord, King Mark, works against us, or he wishes to provoke us into some act of war. Perhaps all three. Be very careful with him. Kay, when you speak to him, guard your tongue."

"I'd prefer not to speak to him at all."

Sir Kay spoke sharply, his words followed at once by Gawain's voice, warm with laughter.

"Kay despises everything from Cornwall, from King Mark down to the inferior breed of fleas on the dogs."

Cautiously, Gareth turned his head to see his brother, his face lit by amusement, and Sir Kay, all cold disdain. Suddenly fearful of catching Gawain's eye, he looked away again, and began assiduously sweeping the hearth.

"Meanwhile," Arthur continued, "we will strengthen the border garrison. "Kay, are the supplies ready?"

"Yes, my lord." Kay was crisply efficient. "The baggage carts are loaded and ready to leave in the morning. A hundred men at arms will ride as escort."

"Good," the king said. "Gawain, you'll take command."

"I'm sure Sir Andret would like to know that," Lancelot remarked.

Gawain laughed. "Of course, he knows already! The man isn't a fool. But there's nothing he can do with what he knows, not while he remains our guest. My lord, we must make our welcome too warm for him to think of leaving."

"The queen has that in hand," Arthur said. "She entertains him now."

Behind him, Gareth heard the shifting of chairs, as if the king had signed for the meeting to end. He began to think that he might as well pick up his basket and go.

Then Sir Kay spoke again. "My lord..." He sounded unusually hesitant. "My lord, may I ride with the escort tomorrow?"

There was a pause; then the king said, "What? No, Kay, I'm sorry. You're needed here."

"But, my lord..." Gareth could hear a note of desperation creep into Kay's voice, though he wondered if any of the others were aware of it. "I've done all that needs doing here," Kay went on painfully. "I – I'm not asking for command, my lord. But I've been all summer behind these walls, and I –"

"I'd be glad of Kay's support," Gawain interposed.

Once again, Gareth risked a look. Kay was leaning forward, hand on the edge of the table, his gaze fixed on Arthur in an almost anguished appeal.

The king was shaking his head. "You're not a child, Kay, to turn away from a tedious duty."

Gareth almost groaned aloud. That was not the way to handle Kay.

Now he sprang to his feet, anger blazing in his eyes, "Is that all you think I'm fit for? Is that what you meant when you accepted my sword and my service?"

Arthur sighed. "Kay, not now. Not when everything is so finely balanced. If things go wrong, we may all need to use our swords."

Kay tossed his hair back. "My lord, you dishonour me!"

At that, Arthur came to his feet slowly, and faced him. "And you, Sir Kay, forget yourself."

"I think there are many things, my lord king, that you have forgotten." Kay's eyes were hot and wretched, focused on Arthur's face. "God forbid that I should ever remind you of them!"

He pressed a hand to his lips, as if he needed to prevent the bitter words from spilling out. Arthur took a step towards him; at that, Kay flinched away, and with a sound in his throat that was half a sob, spun round and almost ran out of the room. With a muttered excuse, Gareth hurried after him.

At the foot of the stairs, a door stood open. Warm lamplight and firelight flooded out into the dark, and the notes of a harp rising over a soft murmur of voices.

It was the door to Queen Guenevere's solar. Gareth, following Sir Kay as he stumbled down the stairs, saw him come to an abrupt stop as he realised he would have to pass through the room on his way out. Watching him, Gareth hesitated at the turn of the stairs.

He saw Kay stand still for a little while, breathing deeply. He passed his hands over his face, and thrust fingers through dishevelled hair. Then, drawing himself up, his step firm enough, he walked through the door.

When Gareth reached it, he saw the queen coming towards Kay, smiling, her hands extended. "Sir Kay, you're the very man I wanted!" Kay, looking awkward, bent over her hand. "Sir Andret has beaten me at chess, and won a jewel from me. And you are the best chess player I know. Will you not challenge him for me?"

Sir Andret was seated in front of a chess table close to the fire, a scatter of pieces in front of him. From one hand he swung a crystal pendant on a silver chain. He wore a smile of smug satisfaction. As Guenevere drew Kay over to him, he half-rose, half-bowed, and his smile broadened.

Guenevere was all laughter, all kindness. Gareth could see that the jewel meant nothing to her, that the suggested game, perhaps, was no more than a way of praising Kay.

Kay himself was reluctant, but incapable of denying her anything. "I'll challenge him gladly, lady," he said, "but I fear I've nothing to stake."

Gareth saw Andret's eyes suddenly narrow; beneath his fox-red hair, his face looked predatory. Gareth caught a hint of danger.

"That ring, perhaps?" Andret suggested.

Kay raised his hand and stared at the ring he was wearing. It was gold, set with a carnelian, incised with the falcon's head that was his device. Dressed in his habitual black, Kay had no other colour about him, and no other ornament. Gareth could not recall that he ever wore another ring than this.

"No, I may not..." he began.

Andret's mouth moved in a sneer. "Have you so little generosity," he said, "that you are afraid to risk a trifle like that to redeem the queen's jewel? Or is Sir Kay as valiant on the chessboard as he is on the battlefield?"

Fury flared in Kay's eyes. He wrenched off the ring and tossed it down beside the chessboard. Then he seated himself in the chair across the board from Andret. "Set up the pieces," he said.

Guenevere was looking troubled at the sudden antagonism between the two men. Glancing around her, at a loss, she saw Gareth hovering beside the open door and beckoned to him. "Do you know what is the matter with Sir Kay?" she asked softly, "I thought only to please him..."

Gareth swallowed nervously, wondering how much he ought to say. "I think that Sir Kay had a... a disagreement with my lord Arthur – no more than can be mended, lady, but..."

Guenevere let out a sigh, and shook her head impatiently. "Oh, Kay!" she sighed. "He is so…" She broke off, perhaps remembering who she was speaking to, and glanced towards the hearth where Sir Andret, playing the white pieces, had just advanced a pawn.

Kay was white-faced, his mouth set. He swiftly countered the move; Andret smiled faintly.

"Oh, no…" Gareth breathed out. He was no chess-player himself, but he knew that the game asked for a cool and logical mind. Kay at his best, he believed loyally, was invincible. But Kay in his present turbulent mood…

"Lady, may I stay?" he asked Guenevere.

Distractedly the queen pushed a bowl of sweetmeats into his hands. "Take those round," she told him. "And keep quiet. If Sir Kay sends you away, you will have to go."

Gareth kept very quiet, padding softly round the room to offer the bowl to Guenevere's women where they sat stitching, or listening to the harper, or gossiping in whispery little voices. No one but the queen herself paid much attention to the game of chess.

At the end of his round of the room, Gareth dared to hold the bowl out to the chess players. Kay, in deep concentration now, waved it away without seeing who held it; Andret chose a sugared fruit with thin, claw-tipped fingers, and went on watching Kay. The queen's jewel flashed fire beside the board, next to the smouldering glow of Kay's carnelian.

Gareth tried to understand how the game was progressing, without much success; the sides seemed evenly matched. He was, as always, fascinated by the pieces, fierce little warriors carved fine as lace. They had come from the East, along with silks and spices, a New Year's gift from Kay himself to the queen.

Gareth returned to Guenevere with the almost empty bowl and looked questioningly at her. She was following the game with almost as much concentration as the players; she was herself very skilled.

"If Kay doesn't make a mistake," she said, "I think he can win."

While she was speaking, Andret's hand swooped over the board, taking one of Kay's pieces. Guenevere drew in her breath, a tiny, anxious sound. Kay looked up, startled, and met a politely inquiring look from Andret.

"What happened?" Gareth whispered.

"That move…" Guenevere was frowning. "I'm almost sure, but I didn't see. I think Andret moved his piece – moved it first, I mean –"

"You mean he cheated?" Gareth, outraged, still had the sense to keep his voice down. "Why doesn't Kay tell him so?"

Guenevere spread her hands helplessly. "How could he be sure? It would be a challenge, and Sir Andret is here to make peace. It could ruin everything…"

Distressed, she watched the two men by the fire. Gareth wondered if all that was going through Kay's mind. It would not be unexpected for him to lose his temper, not thinking what the consequences might be, but Gareth could see that this time at least he had himself under control. Perhaps he remembered the warning Arthur had given him. Colour had risen in his face, and his hands were clenched, but he said nothing, and in a few moments, deliberately, answered Andret's move.

It was, however, the end of the game. A few more exchanges followed, but Kay was clearly hard-pressed, and before long, with a tiny shrug, he tipped over his king, a gesture of resignation. He rose to his feet and bowed. "My thanks, Sir Andret, for a very… instructive game."

Sir Andret also rose; he looked amused. He held the queen's pendant in one hand, and in the other Kay's ring. "Indeed," he agreed. "Most instructive. In fact, Sir Kay, I'm so grateful to you that I will return the queen's jewel."

He held it out to Guenevere and she took it, but her thanks were mechanical. Her gaze was on Kay. When Sir Andret had withdrawn a little she murmured to him, "Kay, I'm so sorry."

Kay bent over her hand again. He was white, stunned, but from somewhere he had mustered an impregnable dignity. "It's of no importance, lady," he said. He hesitated and then added, "I think that Sir Andret will shortly wish to leave. If you could hold him here for… perhaps another half hour, it would be very helpful."

Uncomprehending, Guenevere still agreed.

Kay turned swiftly to Gareth. "Come with me, boy. I've a job for you."

With a correct but hurried leave-taking, he was across the room and out of the far door. Gareth's last impression of the room was of Sir Andret, seated once again by the chess table, flicking Kay's ring lazily into the air, so that the stone caught fire.

In the passage outside, Kay gripped Gareth's wrist. "Listen, boy – that ring bears my device. It's my authority in the castle. That's why –"

"Sir!" Gareth exclaimed, appalled.

"Oh, very well," Kay went on savagely. "Tell me how stupid I've been, but do it later. I want you to go round the servants – speak to as many people as you can, and get them to pass the message on. Trust no one bearing that ring. I'm going to see the Captain of the Guard."

He stood for a moment, not releasing Gareth. The light from the corner of the passage threw strong shadows across him, the wild falcon's face, set and desperate.

"Oh, dear God," he whispered. "How am I going to face the king?"

Gareth sped away on Kay's errand. He felt sick with apprehension at the thought of what Andret could do with the ring; it would give him authority to enter any part of the castle, to give what orders he pleased, until the truth was known. Gareth hoped that the queen would be able to hold Sir Andret at her side.

At last he arrived at the stable yard. It was late; the night was pitch black except for the torches that flared at the postern gate.

As Gareth approached he heard movement in the stables; a door opened, shedding light into the cobbled yard, and a man appeared, quietly leading a horse. Catching his breath, Gareth recognised him: a tall, pale man that he had last seen in Sir Andret's retinue.

He led the horse across the yard to the postern gate, and spoke to the gate-keeper. Gareth waited, expecting him to be turned back.

Instead, after a brief conversation, the gate-keeper saluted and began to raise the bar of the gate.

Gareth started forward. "No! Wait!" he cried.

Andret's servant had already mounted, and snapped something at the gatekeeper, but the man let the bar drop back into its hasps and waited for Gareth to come up.

"What is it, lad?"

"Don't open the gate!" Gareth panted.

"But the man's got an urgent message," the gate-keeper objected. "Sealed by Sir Kay. And his ring for warranty."

Andret's servant thrust out a hand; Gareth saw that he was wearing Kay's carnelian. It took all Gareth's self-control not to try to wrest it away from him.

"The ring was taken from Sir Kay," he explained. "He sent me to –"

"Rubbish!" Andret's servant interrupted. "Sir Kay gave me the ring himself."

In the face of the lie, Gareth was left speechless for a moment, and in that moment the gate-keeper turned away and began to raise the bar again.

"I don't know what you're playing at, lad, he grumbled, "but I don't fancy explaining to Sir Kay why I ignored an order backed by his ring."

As he raised the bar, the messenger pressed forward, trying to thrust his way through the gates the instant they opened. Gareth tried to bar his way. Then a bell began to sound, swift and urgent, the great tocsin on the main gate, and through the peals came shouting and the sound of running footsteps.

Suddenly Kay was there, grasping at the horse's bridle. The horse reared, hooves lashing down. Gareth threw himself backwards, out of range of the thrashing iron, and against the gate, where the gate-keeper, understanding at last, was ready to slot the bar back into position.

It was over. The messenger brought his horse under control. The courtyard seemed full of men-at-arms. And close by, face-down and unmoving, Kay was lying on the stones.

Gareth went to him. He saw again the thrashing hooves that could split a man's head like a ripe fruit. He wanted to be sick.

But as Gareth approached, Sir Kay began trying to get up; Gareth offered him a hand and pulled him to his feet. He was panting, shaken, and blood was trickling from a cut on his forehead.

"Sir!" Gareth exclaimed. "Did the horse —"

"No." Kay gripped Gareth's hand briefly. "I slipped and hit my head. It's nothing. Now —"

Since Gareth had last seen him he had armed himself and now drew his sword. He paced across the yard to where Andret's servant was dismounting. "Now," he said, "we will go and speak to my lord Arthur."

The tocsin was already rousing the court. By the time Gareth, Kay and the messenger reached the wide entrance hall, Arthur was there, approaching down the stairway with Gawain, Lancelot, and others of the knights. Sir Andret was there, too, apparently unmoved by the failure of his plan.

Kay plucked the letter out of the messenger's hand, and took it to the king. While Arthur read it, Kay sheathed his sword again and waited, face like granite. Gareth watched him, and watched the king, his uneasiness growing.

"Details of our reinforcements that will leave tomorrow," Arthur commented at last. "News that King Mark would find very useful. Sealed with your ring, Kay?"

Kay's voice was expressionless, his gaze fixed on nothing. "Earlier tonight, my lord, I lost the ring to Sir Andret, playing chess."

A flicker of some emotion crossed the king's face, as if what Kay said had some significance that Gareth failed to grasp. Arthur said nothing more to Kay, but beckoned to Andret, who stepped forward and bowed, still unperturbed.

"Well?" the king asked.

Andret was collected, even courteous. "I know nothing of the letter, my lord," he said. "As ambassador, I must be neutral. If Sir Kay wished to pass this information on to King Mark, that is his own affair, and I have nothing to say. My servant has, of course, exceeded his duties, and I will reprimand him."

Gareth found that he was driving his nails into his palms. It was a smooth performance, enmeshing Kay in Andret's own treachery. If he had not been present at the chess game, Gareth might even have believed it. No, he told himself, never of Kay.

Kay took a step towards Andret. It seemed as if his stony calm would shatter, but he managed to preserve it. "Then tell me," he asked coldly, "how is it that your servant has the ring? Or do you deny that you won it from me? Do we have to put the queen to the indignity of calling her as a witness?"

Andret was smiling now. He stepped forward, holding out his hands to Kay, as if he offered friendship.

"Kay," he said. "Have you so little courage? You played and lost – and not only at chess. I don't deny that I won the ring, but later, when I realised it was your seal, I returned it to you. Or has that slipped your mind?" He turned his smile, faintly apologetic, on the king; Arthur did not respond. "For trying to involve me, I forgive you," Andret went on, "but there's no hiding it now. I'm sure that for you – his seneschal, almost his brother…" His voice was the flowing of poison wine. "For you, the king will be merciful."

The look Kay gave him was like a brand across his face; Andret stepped back with a tiny shrug. "I've done what I can for you."

For a few seconds it seemed as if the whole assembly was silent, waiting for Kay. The king watched him intently, patiently. Gareth, despairing, realised that Kay had no way of proving that Andret had not returned the ring.

Then Sir Kay spoke. "Sir Andret." His voice was quiet, controlled. "When you say that you returned the ring, you lie. You lie when you say that I wrote the letter. You are a disgrace to knighthood and the office of ambassador. If you wish to prove otherwise, my sword is at your service."

His hand rested on the hilt. There were one or two murmured comments from the watching crowd. Gareth closed his eyes and muttered a prayer.

Sir Andret was looking amused. "A challenge from Sir Kay!" he said. "I am indeed honoured." He snapped his fingers at his servant. "Fetch my sword."

The man bowed and withdrew.

Arthur moved restlessly. "Perhaps tomorrow might be —" he began.

"No!" Andret interrupted sharply, then bowed. "Forgive me, my lord, but I do not wish to sleep with the lie thrown in my face. Unless Sir Kay thinks better of his challenge, we will settle it now."

Kay had already turned away, and was drawing his sword. He stood waiting, head erect, icy. Gareth realised, with a sick sense of dread, how ill Kay must be feeling when he hadn't had time to have his head injury seen to, and he understood why Andret wanted to fight to take place now. He stepped back and murmured to Gawain, who stood close by, "Sir Kay will win, won't he?"

His brother looked at him, his face unusually strained. "I don't know."

"But it's true – everything he said is true!"

Gawain sighed and rested a hand on his shoulder. "Gareth, we might pray to God to defend the right. But so often victory goes to the best fighter."

Andret's servant reappeared, carrying his master's sword. Andret drew it, and weighed the blade in his hand. He was all colour and glitter, set against the more sombre Kay. He bowed ceremonially; Kay responded with a curt inclination of his head. The king gave the signal, and with a swirl of movement from Andret, the fight began.

From the first moments, Gareth's fears were all confirmed. Kay was slow, clumsy; there was no rhythm in his movements. He was struggling to parry the blows of Andret's sword. An expert fighter, like Gawain or Lancelot, might have finished it quickly, but Andret, Gareth began to realise, was no expert. Twice that Gareth could see, he left an opening for Kay, but Kay couldn't take advantage of it; all he could do was defend himself.

The crowd around the edges of the hall were stirring restlessly. There was no spectacle in this fight, no technique to admire, not even the tension of wondering what the outcome would be; all Andret had to do was keep on until he wore down the last of Kay's strength. Gareth heard one or two jeering comments, and a growing murmur that suddenly broke off in a concerted gasp.

Like the flicker of a snake's tongue, so swiftly that Gareth scarcely saw what happened, Andret cast his sword aside and slid forward, under Kay's guard. Another, thinner blade glittered in his hand. Kay, starting back, trying to bring his sword into play, slipped and fell, losing his grip on his own weapon. Andrey sprang on top of him.

A confused murmuring rose once more from the watching crowd. Someone cried, "Treachery!" and Gareth gripped hard on Gawain's arm, unconscious of the pain he must be causing.

Kay and Andret were grappling together. Kay had his fingers clamped around Andret's wrist, forcing the knife downwards until the narrow blade bent against the stone-flagged floor and snapped. Immediately Kay thrust off his enemy, scrambled to his feet and caught up his own sword.

Andret still lay on the floor, momentarily helpless. Gareth cried out, "Now!" but Kay made no move towards his adversary. Instead, he took a pace back, breathing deeply and rubbing the back of his hand against his eyes. He was waiting, as Gareth understood, for Andret to get up and recover his own weapon.

"Does he have to do that?" Gareth asked, anguished.

Gawain made no reply, but was smiling. The smile faded seconds later as Andret made no move to continue the fight.

Instead, he was curled up on the paving stones, his arms shielding his head as if he waited for his death blow. In his own treachery he was incapable of realising that Kay was waiting for him.

Horrible mewling sounds were coming from Andret, gradually formed into coherent words. "No – no!" he gasped out. "I lied – I wrote the letter. Don't…"

He went on babbling, pleas for mercy confused with the details of what he had done so that no one could understand a word of it. Kay just went on staring down at him. Gareth thought he looked as if he wanted to be sick. He was swaying, white with fatigue; he did nothing until the king spoke.

"Kay?"

Kay started, and turned towards Arthur. "My lord?" His voice was shaking. "My lord, what do you want me to do with him?"

"It's your quarrel, Kay," Arthur replied. "Your choice."

Kay went on looking down at the grovelling figure of Andret for a moment longer. Then he said, in such a low voice that only those nearest, like Gareth, could have heard it. "Stop it – get up. No one will harm you. Get up and go."

Without waiting to see what Andret would do, he sheathed his sword and turned away. Before he had taken more than a pace or two, the king called him back.

Kay faced him, but he could do no more. Gareth could see the tension vibrating through him. He was flushed now, his eyes too bright.

Arthur came down to him and took him by the shoulders. "Kay, I can be sure of two things." To Gareth's amazement, the king himself sounded shaken. "Your loyalty, and your… terrible aptitude for trouble."

Kay gazed into his eyes. "Oh, my lord, the ring," he said. His voice was raw with misery. "I didn't mean… I was so sick at heart…"

Arthur's grasp on his shoulders became comforting, almost an embrace. "I know. My fault too, brother. All's right again." He stepped back, releasing Kay. He was smiling. "Go to bed," he said. "You look dreadful."

Kay bowed awkwardly and hurried away.

Gareth at last released his grip on his brother's arm. Gawain flexed it, wincing. "That's my sword arm, you young ruffian."

Gareth grinned at him. He meant to follow Kay and see that his master had a hot bath before going to bed, but then realised there was something more important he could do. "Gawain," he said, "I need your help."

Gareth put a bowl of soup and some bread on a tray, and went to Sir Kay's quarters. He did not bother to knock. The outer room was dark except for a faint glow from a dying fire. Gareth put the tray on the table, wondering if Kay had gone to bed.

A stir of movement drew him over to the fire. On the wooden settle in front of it, Kay was asleep. Gareth stood for a moment, looking down at him. He had obviously pitched down there, exhausted, as soon as he had come in. He had not even bathed the cut on his forehead. Gareth shook his head, with a faint, affectionate smile.

He piled fresh logs on the fire and put the bowl of soup on the hearth to keep warm, before he turned back to Kay. Infinitely careful, not wanting to disturb him yet, he took Kay's hand and slipped the ring onto it, back where it belonged. Waking flames in the fire caught an answering flame from the gold setting, and the carnelian glowed like a tiny sun. The falcon's head, etched in delicate perfection, was as vivid and uncompromising as the face of the man who wore it.

The hand was cold, Gareth covered Kay with his cloak. Then he brought a bowl of water and cleaned the cut; to his relief it was no more than a deep scrape. He had just finished soaking off the last of the dried blood and grit when Kay woke.

He opened his eyes, blinking in bewilderment, trying to focus on Gareth. "Who..? Oh, it's you," he said resignedly. "I might have known."

"How do you feel, sir?" Gareth asked.

Kay half sat up, winced at the movement and lay back again; Gareth managed to slip a cushion behind him.

"My head..." Kay murmured. He raised a hand towards it, and saw the ring.

For a long time he was frozen, staring at it. Gareth didn't dare break the silence. Then with a swift, revealing movement, Kay covered the ring protectively with the other hand. He looked at Gareth. "You did this," he said. "How?"

"I diced with Andret's servant for it," Gareth replied.

Suddenly, treacherously, Kay's mouth quivered, and Gareth turned away to retrieve the bowl of soup.

"I had to borrow some money from Gawain," he said cheerfully, "but I managed to pay it back. He said if he caught me dicing again he would tan my hide with the flat of his sword."

There was no response from Kay, not even the inevitable rebuke when Gareth failed to give a knight his title, until at last he managed to say, stiffly, the words forced out, "Thank you. Not just this. You held the gate. You saved my honour. If the message had reached King Mark..."

Gareth dared to look at him again. Kay was sitting up; his eyes shone and he was trying to smile, as though some warmth within him was struggling to break through the cold exterior.

Gareth returned the smile, trying to show him there was nothing to be ashamed of in revealing himself. He held out the soup. "I brought you some supper, sir."

Kay took the bowl, though he was shivering, and Gareth steadied his hand briefly. He drank with long, shaken breaths, "That's good," he said.

He sat, clasping the bowl, warming his hands on it. He kept giving little glances at the ring, as if afraid it might vanish. After a long time he said, "Arthur gave it to me."

Swift enlightenment dawned on Gareth.

"It was just after he was crowned," Kay went on; his voice had become warm and vibrant, as Gareth had never heard it. "He suddenly realised that he was king, and could give people things. He was so happy doing it. And he gave me this ring." He sighed. "I suppose you think I was very stupid?" He set aside the soup bowl, empty now, and thrust his hands through his hair. He looked exhausted,

"Shall I see you into bed, sir," Gareth offered, rising from the hearth where he had been sitting.

Kay glanced up at him, a faint gleam in his dark eyes. "I'm not senile yet, lad." The gleam vanished; a brief spasm of self-disgust shook him. He spoke half to himself. "How am I going to face everyone tomorrow?"

"You beat Andret, sir," Gareth said encouragingly.

Kay shook his head. "What honour is there in that? A treacherous snake like Andret? A man who can't even play a clean game of chess." His mouth twisted in a bitter smile. "If he had fought fairly, he would have won, for I could not have kept on for much longer."

Yet you still waited for him to pick up his sword, Gareth thought. Aloud, he said, "You were hurt, sir."

"And you think anyone will care about that?" Kay's voice was harsh, castigating himself. "No. They'll only remember that I... I risked the king's trust. For a game of chess."

His head was bowed; the fine hands were clenched together, the carnelian ring glowing in the firelight, the heart of warmth in the wasteland. He was closed in on himself again, struggling with his pain.

Gareth stood looking down at him. He did not know what to do. If you were a kitchen boy, you could not comfort the High Seneschal of Britain, even if you knew that what he needed most was to release himself to someone who cared for him.

If Gawain were here... Gareth thought helplessly. But he was not Gawain, and never would be.

He thought that Kay had forgotten him, until he half turned his head and said brusquely, "It's late, boy. Go to bed."

For a little longer Gareth hesitated, but there was nothing more that he could say, nothing more than a sad, "Good night," as he left the room and closed the door behind him.

Hunt of the Hart Royal

"Look!" said Gareth of Orkney.

Sir Kay, riding just ahead of him, reined in. Their path wound along the side of a hill, and across the valley the forest reached towards them like the fingers of a spread hand. Camelot was an airy silhouette on the horizon.

Gareth pointed. Along the edge of the forest was a glitter of movement: horses, with riders gaily dressed, some followers on foot, and hunting dogs. As Kay and Gareth watched, they heard a horn, faint and clear, and within minutes the whole troop had disappeared among the trees.

"King Arthur hunts the white stag," Kay said.

His tone was indifferent, and he urged his horse forward again. Gareth followed, pressing up as closely as he could on the narrow path.

"A white stag!" he said, marvelling. "Sir, is there really such a thing?"

"Oh, yes. I've seen one myself. And I've no wish to see this one." Now he sounded irritable. "Do you know the custom of the hunt?"

"No," Gareth said.

"The knight who kills the white stag," Kay instructed him, glancing over his shoulder with a sardonic look, "has the honour of kissing the most beautiful lady in the court."

Gareth shrugged; he could think of prizes more exciting. "I suppose..." he began.

Kay paused again at a turn of the path. "You don't see the point, lad, do you? What red-blooded knight doesn't think his own lady is most beautiful, and wouldn't challenge anyone who says different? Last time, I thought we'd have a massacre on our hands."

Gareth began to understand. "Why does Arthur do it, then?"

Kay's brows went up, disdain in his hawk's face. "Custom. To entertain his guests. Honour." He reached out, soothing his black Morial as the horse grew restive. Now he was Kay at his most sarcastic. "If we hear tell of something wonderful, what else should we do but kill it?"

He moved on. Behind him, Gareth, half smiling, thought that even his back view looked disgusted, from crisp black curls to polished riding boots. Impossible to imagine Sir Kay contending for the prize of a kiss.

Kay and Gareth had left Camelot at dawn to visit nearby farms, paying for provisions supplied for the recent Easter Court, and giving orders for the approaching Court at Pentecost. Gareth had assumed that Kay had undertaken the errand himself, instead of sending one of his staff, to avoid the exasperating influx of noble visitors. Now he guessed that Kay might also have wanted to avoid the hunt.

At each of the farms on their route, Kay would have long and complicated discussions with the farmer, involving money and tally-sticks. Afterwards would come a stroll around outside, to look at pigs or chickens or fields of green corn.

Kay listened more than he talked, seemingly consumed by interest in the ingredients of a horse drench or why certain hens were failing to lay. Not until Gareth saw him crouched in a cow byre, encouraging a calf to drink from a bucket, the little creature determined to suck down his fingers along with the milk, did he realise that Kay was not pretending interest at all. Strangely, he belonged here in a way that he did not belong at Camelot.

Once they were on their way again, Kay said, abrupt and self-conscious, "I was brought up to this. My father's tenants. But for Arthur I might have spent my whole life watching wool grow on sheep." As Gareth considered this new idea – for he could scarcely imagine Kay separated from the office of High Seneschal – Kay added, "I could milk a cow before I learned to use a sword." He released a spurt of laughter, touched with bitterness. "There are those who would say I should have stuck to milking."

All day they rode in a wide circle, with Camelot at its centre, so that when they left the last farm they were still less than an hour's ride from home. The sun was sinking, their shadows growing long.

"The quickest road goes through the forest," Kay said, gesturing. His mouth quirked. "You might even see your stag."

Gareth felt anticipation quicken. A white stag; might it still be concealed among the brakes and thickets, or would the hunt have found it and pulled it down? He swallowed uncomfortably; he would rather not see that.

In the forest, all was quiet. The sunlight was reddening, the shadows of the trees lying across their path. There was no disturbance of the track or the undergrowth to show the hunt had ever been this way. Very faintly, Gareth could hear running water.

As they went on, the sound grew louder; the path was descending and growing damp. Concentrating on his horse's footing, Gareth was not aware that Kay had reined in until he came up beside him, and Kay's hand reached out to his bridle.

"Listen."

Now that the horses were standing, Gareth could hear splashing from the water he still could not see, as if something large was wallowing around. From the distance came the call of a hunting horn.

Kay dismounted, looped Morial's reins over a low branch, and strode into the long grasses beside the track, vanishing as he skirted a hazel brake. Hurrying after him, Gareth started to call out, and bit off the words as he caught up.

The stream ran in a deep cleft, the banks undercut. Kay knelt on the edge; directly beneath him was the stag. It stood shoulder-deep in water, its forelegs pawing at the bank, which crumbled away as it tried to lever itself upwards. Its head was lifted, close enough for Gareth, crouching at Kay's side, to have reached out and touched, until the animal fell back in a surge of water.

When Kay had told him about the white stag, Gareth had not fully understood the wonder of it. The hide was the same pure silver as the water that bubbled around it; wet, it had the sheen of silk. The antlers were frozen light. Gareth wanted to hide his eyes, and yet he could not stop looking.

Kay breathed out, "It's wounded."

As the stag struggled upwards again, Gareth saw the gashes along its flank, ugly gaping mouths where blood flowed, mingling with the stream. An arrow was deep in its neck; it mouth was flecked with blood-stained foam. Once again it fell back, and this time the current carried it off its feet and threw it up against the bank further downstream.

Gareth heard the horn call again, and the distant yelping of a hound. He understood what had happened. The stag had taken to the water to break the scent; the huntsmen had lost it, but it was too badly wounded to escape. It would die, and not easily, from drowning or loss of blood.

Uncertainly, Gareth glanced at Kay, wondering if there was anything they could do. Kay was looking white and sick. Still with his eyes fixed on the struggling animal, he unfastened his cloak and let it fall. Then he drew his dagger, the only weapon he was wearing.

Gareth exclaimed, "Sir, you can't! Wait for the hunt."

"The hunt, lad?" Kay's vice was scathing. "I might wait all night."

Without hesitating, he swung himself off the edge of the bank. Gareth watched, agonised. The water ran deep enough to drown in, as well as the danger of being injured by the stag's thrashing hooves or its antlers.

Kay slithered down the bank into the water, and let the current take him. The stag was pawing at the bank again, but already Gareth could see that it was weaker. Kay was driven against its flank, a dark, drenched shape against the glimmering silver, reached for its shoulder and drew himself upwards. The stag turned its head and looked at him.

Briefly, Kay froze. Then he poised his hand, gripping the dagger, hesitated, then plunged the blade into the vein at the base of the stag's neck. Blood gushed out, over the stag's chest, over Kay's hand, to be lost in the swirling water.

The light in the antlers died; they were only horn, the colour of rancid fat. The gleaming hide grew dingy. The body slipped down the bank, only the head and one shoulder exposed, all the marvel of it dissolving away. It was nothing more than a dead animal.

Kay's grip slackened on the hilt of the dagger. He slid back, leaving the weapon buried in the stag's neck, and water closed over his head.

Terrified, Gareth scrambled along the bank, ready to go in after him, when he saw Kay's head break surface. "Kay!" he cried.

Kay heard him, but he looked dazed, as if he had forgotten what to do. Gareth lay flat and reached an arm down to him, but the bank was too high. Clumsy in his haste, he tore off the belt of his tunic and let it hang down. This time Kay managed to clutch it. Gareth drew him in under the bank until he could stand, then caught his wrists and hauled him out. He was dazed still, shuddering, and collapsed on the edge of the overhang. Gareth took him by the shoulders and dragged him into safety.

He did not realise until then that the hunt had drawn closer. The horn again; the baying of hounds; the crashing of horses in the undergrowth. Gareth looked up, over Kay's huddled body, and saw the riders pushing through the trees into the open space on the far bank. King Arthur was the foremost of them.

The king dismounted and strode to the edge of the stream. For a moment he stood still, looking down at the dead stag.

"Kay!" he said. Kay raised his head. "Kay, if you wished to win the prize, it would become you better to have joined the hunt. There is no honour in stealing another man's kill." Kay flinched at the tone, but said nothing. "Follow us back to court," Arthur ordered.

Unsteadily, Kay rose to his feet. His voice rasped in his throat. "My lord, I –" he broke off. His head went up, inflexible pride meeting Arthur's hostility. Mouth tightening, he turned and stumbled back towards the horses.

Gareth stared across the stream at the huntsmen, the horses milling around in the confined space, the bright clothes of their riders breaking up the greens of the forest. Kay refused to defend himself; Gareth wanted to do it for him, to explain that Kay had killed the stag out of mercy, not to steal the prize, but he knew Arthur would not listen. Here Gareth was no more than a kitchen boy, Kay's servant, too insignificant to speak to kings. He caught up Kay's discarded cloak and followed him.

There was light still in the sky when the company reached Camelot. Kay and Gareth rode through the gates of the citadel last of all. Inside, among the horses and huntsmen, Arthur was waiting. He stood alone, a little space around him. "Kay," he said.

His voice was quiet, but it carried. Kay approached and dismounted, but remained clinging to the bridle. Gareth suspected that was all that kept him on his feet.

"Kay," King Arthur said, "don't fail to be at supper tonight. We're all eager to see you claim the prize for your kill."

In the crowd, someone laughed. Kay drew in a gasping breath, said, "But I –" and stopped. He faced Arthur. His black hair was plastered to his head, streaked against a face white as bone. His clothes were sodden from the stream. He was still refusing to justify himself.

"As you will, my lord," he said.

Arthur contemplated him. There was something between the two men, fierce as swords. The king could not allay it. Without another word, he turned and went inside.

At once the knights began to press around Kay.

"Give the kiss to my lady, Kay," one said. "Or meet me in combat tomorrow."

"Kiss my lady, Kay, or feel my sword."

"Give it to my lady."

"No, to mine."

At last Gareth understood. Kay had no lady of his own, no reason to choose any of the court ladies over another. But whoever he chose, the other knights would challenge him, to defend their lady's beauty, or simply to win an easy victory. Kay was no fighter, and his sharp tongue had made him unpopular. Plenty of men would be glad to see him humiliated. Kay's only choices were to decline the prize and be branded a coward, or fight combat after combat until he was seriously wounded, or killed. Now he stood silent, mouth set, eyes parrying the mocking threats. Gareth's heart twisted in pity.

As the crowd thinned out, another figure approached Kay, tall, dark, grave-faced: Lancelot. "Kay," he said. Kay's head snapped round to face him. "Kay," Lancelot went on, "give the kiss to the queen. If anyone dares challenge, I will answer. It is my right; I am Queen's Champion."

It was a way out, but almost before Lancelot had finished speaking, Kay was replying, a cutting edge to his words.

"Does your sword grow rusty, Sir Lancelot? Or have you not honour enough? Would it please you if they said Kay cowered behind your shield? No. I fight my own battles."

Before his quivering fury, Lancelot inclined his head and moved away, his gravity undisturbed. Gareth saw Kay's taut defiance begin to relax, only to gather again as another man came up: Gareth's own brother, Sir Gawain.

Gareth drew closer, listening eagerly, irrationally beginning to hope. Gawain was smiling faintly, and held out a hand, but Kay ignored it.

"I'm sorry, Kay," Gawain said. "I know you never meant this. Listen – do as Lancelot says, and give the kiss to the queen. There'll be challenges, but we'll meet them together – you and I, and Lancelot, Gaheris – and I'll find some others. We'll fight a melee. We'll do it to entertain the guests."

Gareth was grinning delightedly at Gawain's solution, until he saw Kay shake his head. He was not hostile, as he had been to Lancelot; Gareth thought that Gawain's courtesy had almost broken him, but he was still refusing.

"I cannot, Sir Gawain," he said. "I must face it alone. There are those who will brand me coward, who would not dare say such a thing of Gawain of Orkney. But I thank you."

Gawain hesitated, and then touched his arm. "Tell me if you change your mind," he said, and was gone.

Kay stood with his face turned away into Morial's neck. He was shivering in the evening chill. Gareth was afraid that he was weeping. He took a tentative step forward.

"They rejoice to see me shamed," Kay choked out. "Even the king."

"Not Gawain," Gareth said instantly.

"No, not Gawain."

The words were sighed out. Kay's shoulders drooped. Gareth went to him, wanting to get him inside before he collapsed in front of the grooms. He needed a bath and a change of clothes; even then he would not be fit to face the ordeal in the Great Hall.

Before Gareth could touch him, Kay straightened. There were no tears on his face, but he had a wild, desperate look that terrified Gareth.

"I'll not endure it," he said. "Everyone spits on my name. Arthur scorns my service. I'll go, and end it."

As he spoke, he mounted again, and gathered Morial's reins.

"No!" Gareth cried, appalled. "Sir, they'll call you coward. You won't be able to come back! Sir, listen to me, go and talk to Gawain –"

He was speaking to empty air. Kay was already thrusting Morial through the gate. Gareth flung himself into the saddle and followed.

He tracked Kay through the city by the sharp sound of Morial's hooves on the cobbles. Kay was unaware of him, but at the city gate he had to wait for the guards to open it, and Gareth managed to come up with him.

"Sir, don't –" he gasped out.

"Go away!" Kay snapped, and urged Morial out into the gathering darkness.

Ignoring his order, Gareth still followed, but once through the gate Kay's horse leapt forward, arrow-swift. Despairingly, Gareth spurred his own horse into a gallop, but he knew that this stocky chestnut had no hope of catching Morial.

Kay was returning the way they had come. The road crossed the valley, breasted the hill beyond, and followed the edge of the forest. In the last, dim streaks of daylight, Gareth lost sight of Kay. He wondered whether to go back, find Gawain, beg him for help, but by then Kay could be miles away, lost.

At length the road turned under the trees. Gareth had to check his horse, but he began to hope again, for he knew that Kay would do the same. He would never risk laming Morial by a wild gallop in darkness.

Soon Gareth began to hear sounds in front of him. He pressed forward as fast as he dared, until he came out into a long forest ride, sloping down towards the stream. Not far ahead he could see Kay.

"Sir!" he called. "Wait for me!"

Kay halted and pulled Morial round. As Gareth approached, he said roughly, "I told you to go away."

"I can't leave you, sir," Gareth said. "What will you do, alone? You're not even armed. You –"

Kay interrupted him. "Go back. You can't help me."

"Come back with me, then," Gareth urged him. "You're High Seneschal, sir. You can't throw it all away. Talk to Gawain, and –"

At first he thought Kay was wavering, but the mention of Gawain had been a mistake. Kay's hands clenched on the reins. "No," he said.

"Then I'm coming with you," Gareth said.

Kay stared at him. "Don't be a fool, boy," he said. "Your life is there, in Camelot. They'll make you knight at Pentecost. You'll belong."

"I'm not going back," Gareth said steadily. He dared reach out and take hold of Morial's bridle. "Not without you."

He was not sure himself why he offered the sacrifice. Most of the knights probably thought that he hated Kay, and with good reason, when Kay had put him to work in the kitchens. Gareth was not used to analysing himself, but he knew that hatred was the last thing he felt. And somehow, without having the words to express it, he knew that Camelot would not be Camelot if it had no place for a man such as Kay.

If Gareth had wanted to explain himself, there was no time. Kay wrenched the bridle out of his grasp. The wild look was back in his eyes. "In God's name, leave me alone!" he cried.

Before Gareth could answer, another voice rang out like the note of a bell. "Sir Kay."

Kay's head whipped round. A few yards further down the ride was a bridge across the stream, not far from where Kay had killed the stag. On this bridge stood a lady.

Afterwards, Gareth found it hard to describe her. She was not young, nor beautiful. Her hair was dark, and her eyes, and she wore a blue mantle. Her face held such deep serenity that he thought he might drown in it.

With a dazed look, Kay walked Morial towards the bridge. There he dismounted, and went down on one knee. "Lady," he said. "What do you want with me?"

"I need a knight's service," she replied.

A shaken laugh escaped Kay. He gestured down the road. "There lies Camelot, lady," he said, "where the best knights in the world will vie to serve you. You have no need of Kay."

The lady's gaze remained gravely on him. "Sir Kay, this task is yours," she said.

She drew a cup from the folds of her mantle, and held it out to him. It was a plain chalice, made of pewter, Gareth guessed, or possibly silver. If he had seen it on a table in the Great Hall he would have passed it without a second glance, but here it seemed to have gathered to itself all the light that remained as the forest drew towards the dark.

"Fill this cup from the source of the stream," the lady said, "and bring it here to me. Do this, and I will tell you how to fulfil the custom of the hunt at Arthur's feast tonight."

Terror clawed at Gareth. Who was the lady, how could she know Kay's desperate need, unless through sorcery, or something deeper than sorcery? All his instincts told him to turn and flee, but instead he dismounted and came to stand beside Kay.

Kay was looking up at the lady with a swift hope lighting his face. "I will try," he said, and took the cup from her. Briefly he looked startled, as if it was heavier than he expected.

"You answer well," the lady said, "for the task is not as simple as it seems."

"May I help him?" Gareth asked.

Kay, still kneeling, gave him a fierce look, but the lady smiled. "You may go with him," she said, "for your heart is faithful and brave, but the task is Kay's alone, if he wishes to win the reward. Meet me here, Sir Kay, when it is done."

Kay rose, and bowed. Somehow, without Gareth's seeing exactly how, the lady withdrew into the shadows. Kay stood gazing down into the cup, and without being told Gareth unsaddled Morial so that the horse could graze.

When he began to do the same with his chestnut, Kay said, "I don't need a nursemaid, boy." But he made no protest when Gareth followed him along the bank of the stream.

Soon they passed the place where the stag had died. Gareth could still see where the horses had trampled the grass, and the scars on the bank where the stag had struggled, but of the body there was no sign. Gareth could not remember seeing the huntsmen carrying in their kill.

He was worrying about something more practical: how long it would take to reach the source of the stream. Even if the lady told Kay how to answer the challenge, it would be useless if Kay was late returning. By now the light had almost gone; they groped forward with only the sound of the stream as a guide.

Then Gareth began to make out Kay's dark form ahead of him, outlined in faint, silvery light. It was like moonlight, but moonrise remained hours away. Only gradually, as the light strengthened, did Gareth realise that it came from the cup.

Radiance struck out from the vessel, frosting the grass and brambles that overhung the path. It caught the branches of the trees above, so that they looked like the vaulting of some great cathedral. Kay and Gareth walked up an aisle flanked by living columns, where light drizzled down like rain. The cup itself had grown too dazzling for Gareth to look at, and he half believed that it must sear the flesh from Kay's hands. Kay moved like a man in a dream.

At last they came to a wall of tumbled rock, where the stream poured out above their heads. Kay halted and looked up.

The light blanched his features, cruelly revealing the lines of strain. He was near exhaustion. But after a second's pause, without a word or even a glance at Gareth, he reached out to grip the rock and began to climb.

Gareth watched anxiously. One-handed, carrying the cup, Kay was slow and clumsy. If he fell, he might injure himself, when injury meant failure and a self-imposed exile.

He reached the source at last and leant over precariously, clutching a spur of rock, to fill the cup. As the stream splashed in the water itself received the radiance and fell like molten silver from a crucible, veining the rock beneath, until the pool at its foot brimmed with incandescent light.

Kay drew back and began to edge his way down. He slid the last foot or two to the ground, staggering and barely saving the cup. Light splashed over his hands as Gareth steadied him by the shoulders. Kay shrank into himself, as if he still could not admit Gareth was there.

The brilliance of the falls died behind them as they returned, until their way was lit only by the cup between Kay's hands. Gareth became aware of tiny flickering movements at the edge of sight, but if he jerked his head round there was nothing. He felt uneasily that he preferred not to see what had been there. At the same time, he began to sense an oppressive weight overhead, as if the sky had suddenly clamped down at the level of the trees. The air seemed taut as a bowstring; it became hard to breathe. The forest was silent except for their footsteps, yet the silence itself howled a malediction. Darkness pressed in on the fragile sphere of light shed by the cup, as if it could burst it like a bubble.

Kay was glancing swiftly from side to side, or up at the canopy, now drowned in darkness. Gareth heard his breathing grow harsh and shallow. He carried the cup as if its weight was almost too great to bear. At last he stumbled to a stop and stood shivering.

Gareth knew that he himself had been lightly brushed by the edge of the mystical pattern that played itself out in the forest. Kay was enmeshed more deeply in the heart of it, and the assault they endured now was hurled more savagely against him.

Daringly, Gareth slid an arm around him. "Sir?" he said.

Gasping for breath, Kay leant back against his shoulder. "Go — if you can," he said. "Take the cup."

"But it's your task, sir. The lady said so."

"You must do it. I can't. I am not... worthy."

He was trying to give the cup to Gareth. Light spattered out of it. In another minute he would drop it; unprotected, the dark would crush them. With his free hand, Gareth steadied the cup, but he would not take it.

He tightened his hold on Kay and urged him gently forward, half-supporting him, so that all Kay had to do was keep the cup from spilling. A few paces like this, and then Kay shook his head as if to clear it and drew himself erect. The look he gave Gareth, mingled shame and gratitude and a kind of derisive resolve, almost made Gareth weep.

Now Kay went on more firmly; it did not seem long before they came to the bridge where the lady waited.

"Welcome," she said.

As she spoke, the tightness in the air was scattered. The unheard voices sank into true silence. The huge, immanent presence overhead lifted and was gone. Gareth felt that he could raise his head and draw a clean breath that became a gasp of astonishment. Beyond the lady, twilight still glimmered along the ride, as if no time had passed since the three of them last stood there.

Kay walked forward, holding the cup, bearing it easily now. "I have what you asked for, lady," he said.

The lady smiled and took the cup from him. "You have done well, sir," she said. "And now come with me and see a wonder."

She led them along the opposite bank of the stream until they came to a clearing. Gareth was not surprised to see the stag there, lying dead among the creeping foliage of the forest floor.

The lady held the cup over the stag's head and tilted it. Liquid light poured out and splashed between the antlers. Beneath it the velvet brow glimmered silver; trickles of silver began to creep down the muzzle, the neck, along the curve of the antlers. The trickles grew, spread, ran one into another, until a tide of silver swept across the body, until it shone as Gareth had first seen it.

Old scars seamed the side where the wounds had gaped. The flank rose and fell gently in a regular rhythm. The eyes opened. An anguished cry, stifled almost at once, tore from Kay.

The stag raised one foreleg, then the other, and surged to its feet. The antlers laced the forest darkness like the ripple of moonlight on water. The watchers stood in the circle of quiet radiance.

"What was dead, lives," the lady said. "What was lost is restored. All pain is healed." She smiled at Kay. "And now, sir, your reward."

She drew close to Kay, and spoke softly to him. Gareth could not hear the words, but he could see the change in Kay: the sudden light springing into his face, the indrawn breath that became a spasm of shocked laughter.

Then as he gazed into the lady's face, all laughter dissolved in awe, and he fell to his knees. The lady raised the cup, and reached out her other hand to him in a sign of blessing.

On their return to Camelot, Kay went to bathe and change, while Gareth was caught up in the final turmoil of preparing for the feast.

When he went up to serve in the Great Hall, he looked vainly for Kay. The first course was on the table before the seneschal made his entrance.

It was an entrance. Tonight Sir Kay, an austere man, had dressed magnificently in a blue velvet robe, the high collar stiff with silver thread. He stalked down the length of the hall, dragging silence after him, and stood before Arthur with his head high. Gareth edged closer.

"My lord," Kay said, "I am here as you commanded, to take the prize for the kill."

By now, Arthur's anger had ebbed; he was looking uneasy. "Are you sure, Kay?" he asked. "Do you want more time to think?"

It was an overture of friendship, perhaps an offer of help, but Kay rejected it with all the arrogance of an untamed hawk. "I have made my choice, my lord."

He was quite white, except for a hectic flush on his cheekbones. Gareth had seen him like this before, so tense you could have strung a bow with him. There was nothing Gareth could do except pray that no one would goad him into losing that precarious self-control.

Kay turned his back on the dais, and faced the company in the body of the hall, the knights and their ladies, the guests who had stayed on after the Easter Court, the squires, pages and servants.

"I have made my choice," he repeated. "A choice that no one in this hall will quarrel with."

His confidence held them silent for a brief moment, until someone called out, "I claim quarrel, Kay, unless you choose my lady."

Clamour erupted; some of the knights leapt to their feet. To Gareth's relief, Kay held himself aloof, showing nothing but a faint disdain. He spoke to Arthur. "With your leave, my lord…"

Arthur nodded.

Kay beckoned to Gareth. "Boy, bring me the king's shield from the wall."

With an effort, Gareth stopped himself from gawking, and went to do Kay's bidding. Arthur's shield hung behind his seat, at the back of the dais, the shields of his knights alongside it. As Gareth stretched to lift it down, he began to understand. A tight knot of excitement grew in his stomach.

He carried the shield to where Kay was waiting. By this time, Arthur had imposed silence again.

"The hall is filled with fair ladies," Kay said. "So beautiful that I should not presume to judge. Yet there is another more beautiful still, and she must be my choice."

He stepped forward and touched his lips to the icon of the Mother of God that Arthur bore on his shield.

The hall had been quiet before; now it was as if all sound had been wiped away with a sponge. Kay moved away from the shield and looked around. A gleam of triumph shone in his eyes. "Do I hear a challenge?" he asked.

There was no reply. Kay turned to the king, with a faintly inquiring look.

Arthur smiled, reluctantly. "No challenge, Kay," he said. He waved a hand at Gareth. "Put it away, boy."

As Gareth returned the shield to its place, a babble broke out; he heard Bedivere saying, "Was that blasphemous, or just damn' clever?"

Gareth smiled to himself, but the smile faded as he turned back and saw Kay bowing to the king as if he meant to leave.

"Don't go, Kay," the king said. "Take your place with us."

Kay drew himself up. His air of triumph had gone, leaving only that indomitable pride. *No!* Gareth willed him. What was the good of pride, if all it led to was cold and loneliness and a bitter brooding? Kay had borne the cup; he had endured all the force of that evil assault; he had seen the wonder of the stag. None of these others, not even King Arthur himself, could understand that, but they could not be blamed for it. The last pain would not be truly healed unless Kay could dare to be reconciled.

There was an empty place at the High Table, close to Arthur. Gawain, seated beside it, made a tiny gesture of invitation. Kay raised a hand to his throat, as if he could not breathe. He made no move, but when Gawain rose and guided him to the seat, he did not resist. He sat with eyes cast down, and Arthur leant across the table towards him, speaking earnestly.

Gareth let out a long sigh of relief, and went to fetch a jug to pour wine for his lord.

The Avowing of Sir Kay

Gareth of Orkney, a wine flagon in each hand, mounted the stair towards King Arthur's private rooms. The Easter Court was over, though many of the knights and guests would stay until the greatest court of the year at Pentecost.

And at Pentecost, Gareth reflected, he could say goodbye to carrying wine flagons, scrubbing floors, and all the other tasks of a kitchen boy at the court of Camelot. At Pentecost he would be made knight.

What would he be, he wondered, how would he change, when at last he felt the touch of the accolade? As he manoeuvred his way through the door, awkwardly because of the flagons he carried, he asked himself how it would feel, to be a Knight of the Round Table, to share that glittering reputation and uphold it in the sight of the whole world.

Inside the room, King Arthur sat at a small table near the fire, in front of a chess board, though the pieces were scattered, the game over. Opposite him was Sir Kay the Seneschal, twirling one of the black chess knights between his fingers.

Others of the company were seated around them. Sir Ector de Maris, on his feet but none too steady, his wine cup in his hand, spoke with stately deliberation.

"I vow to leave Camelot tomorrow and seek out monsters. Dragons, cockatrices, amphisbaenas. I vow I will slay all I find, and return with their heads at Pentecost."

"Praise God!" Sir Kay's words were no more than a satirical murmur. "I'll sleep easier in my bed now."

Gareth of Orkney hid a smile. A Knight of the Round Table, of course, was never drunk, but when they had been drinking they often hatched some very strange ideas.

He set down one of the flagons on a side table, and went round with the other, filling cups.

"Sir Kay," Lancelot said with his usual measured gravity – he was not drunk, nor ever would be – "it ill becomes you to make mock of another knight's vow. For my part, I vow to ride with my brother Ector, and aid him, and lay my trophies at the Queen's feet."

"Better hire a cart," Kay said.

Any response Sir Lancelot might have made was interrupted by Gaheris, who sprang to his feet eagerly. "I vow to keep the ford by Astolat, and challenge all strange knights who wish to pass."

"I'll ride north," Bedivere said. "Slaughter a few damn' Saxons."

Arthur had listened thoughtfully to all of this, and was beginning to look faintly troubled. "Make what vows you wish," he said. "I honour my knights' courage. But think well. I would not lose you over a game such as this."

Gareth finished his round of the wine cups, and set the flagon down. By now the knights were so intent on the game of vows that they did not notice he was there. Just to be sure they would not send him away, he knelt in the hearth and began to build up the fire.

Sir Gawain spoke, soft-voiced as always. "My lord, I will not leave the court before Pentecost. But I vow myself to the service of any lady who asks for aid."

A wise vow, Gareth thought. It was no more than Gawain was ready to do every day of his life.

Sir Kay let out a crack of laughter. "I'll find you a flail, Gawain, to beat them off."

Sir Gawain chose to join in Kay's laughter, leaching out its bitterness.

By now Sir Bors had risen to his feet, and pledged Arthur before he said, "I vow to keep vigil in the cathedral each night until Pentecost, and banish any demons that may assail me."

"Demons?" Contempt glittered in Sir Kay's eyes. "Surely, Bors, no self-respecting demon would dare come within a hundred miles of you?"

"Sir Kay!" It was Lancelot who replied, anger now in the grave voice. "You sneer at good knights, but what achievements can you show to match theirs? Unless knighthood has become a matter of kitchen slops and account books, instead of battle and glory."

Sir Kay rose to his feet, his hawk's face fierce. "If it was not for the kitchen slops and account books, Lancelot, you would find little comfort here in Camelot when you come back from seeking glory."

Lancelot's anger intensified, focused on Kay. He ignored Sir Gawain, who tried vainly to interrupt.

"A knight who values comfort is no true knight," he said. "I would prove that with my sword, Sir Kay, but that we are companions of the Table. If that did not protect you, you would not dare speak as you do."

"I dare to meet you." Kay's words flashed out. "Or do you –"

"You would not dare." Lancelot overbore him. "You will not even take part in this knightly game of vows."

The atmosphere in the room was crackling as fiercely as the flames seizing the fresh logs Gareth had laid on them.

"Very well." Kay drained his wine cup and set it down on the table with a sharp sound in the sudden silence. "I vow that I will ride from here and take the adventure God sends me. And I will not return until I have done a greater deed than any of you."

"Kay!" Arthur exclaimed, appalled.

Kay sent a scalding glance around the room. He said nothing more, but turned his back on the king and his knights, and went out.

Gareth put soup, bread and cold meat onto a tray, along with a jug of good wine, and took it to Sir Kay's rooms. Kay was hunched up on the settle, staring into the last embers of the fire, looking like a falcon in moult. He had not drunk too much that evening, Gareth realised. Sir Kay did not need to drink to get himself into trouble; he could do it perfectly well sober.

Gareth deliberately made a noise, banging the door behind him and thumping the tray down on the table. "Supper, sir," he said.

Kay waved a hand impatiently, not looking at him. "Take it away."

"You didn't eat in the hall, sir."

This time Sir Kay turned and frowned at Gareth over the back of the settle. "The trouble with you, boy, is you think I need a nursemaid."

Without replying, Gareth poured a cup of wine, took it to Kay and presented it, kneeling. Kay took it, only muttering, "You're not in the great hall now."

He stared into the cup but did not drink. Gareth stayed on his knees. "Sir," he said dramatically, "I crave a boon."

"Get up, boy," Kay snapped. "Stop fooling around. What boon? Don't think I'm going to promise anything unless I know what it is. I've made enough rash vows for one night."

"I want to come with you, sir."

Kay's eyes sharpened. With a sudden chill, Gareth realised he had overstepped the boundary into the place where Kay allowed no one else to enter.

"No," Kay said. "Get out." When Gareth did not move, he added, "Do you want to hold my hand, or make sure I keep my feet dry? I told you, boy, I don't need a nursemaid."

"But a knight may need a squire, sir."

"You?" Kay cocked a brow at him. "They'll make you knight at Pentecost, boy. But for that you must be here."

Before Gareth could reply, there was a soft tap on the door. Gareth sprang to his feet and bowed as King Arthur entered. Kay rose, too, hesitantly; his face was blanched as if death had laid a finger on it.

"Kay?" Arthur strode across the room and grasped the seneschal's shoulders. "Kay, you don't mean to leave tomorrow?"

Kay's mouth set in a stubborn line. "I must, my lord."

"This vow of yours – I'll release you from it. There's no need to –"

"And have me called oathbreaker?"

Arthur went on looking down at him for a moment, his expression a mixture of understanding and exasperation. He half smiled, but for some reason the look made Gareth feel like weeping, and Kay averted his face.

"No one will shame you in my hearing," Arthur said.

"But you are not always there to hear. Do you know what they speak of Kay? Arrogant, cowardly, discourteous… but no one can say that I ever broke my word."

He tried to pull away from Arthur, who resisted, and drew him, unwillingly, into an embrace. "Kay, there will always be a place for you here," he said, and went out.

Kay sank down on the settle and put his head in his hands. Gareth remained where he was, in silence. Something told him this was not the time to offer comfort, or repeat his request.

After a moment Kay said, his voice scarcely above a whisper, "You know that I can never fulfil my vow? You know that I can never come back?"

"Yes." Like it or not, Gareth knew that was what Kay believed.

"Then…" he was struggling for words. "Then you may ride with me, if you promise to return before Pentecost."

Gareth always found it hard to be properly miserable, even in the freezing depths of winter. It was even harder now, as he rode out from Camelot the next morning, with sunlight dappling the ground beneath the trees and flowers studding the grass. Now he felt like adding his own whistling to the birdsong. The sight of Sir Kay riding a pace or two ahead of him in sombre silence, was enough to stifle the impulse.

When Gareth had first come to Camelot, almost a year before, he had not told his name. He had asked to serve in the court for a year, and Sir Kay the Seneschal had put him to work in the kitchens.

The decision had scandalised the other knights. A nobly born youth could not be expected to get his hands dirty.

Yet Gareth was content. Sir Kay, for whatever reason, had given him what he wanted. Gareth had come to appreciate his sarcasm instead of being intimidated by it. And he had begun to have some idea of the demons that drove the seneschal.

They rode through the forest. As far as Gareth could see, Kay was choosing paths at random. From time to time Gareth thought he heard sounds as if at least one other horseman was following them, or pacing them through the trees, but he could see nothing. Perhaps, he thought, it was Sir Ector looking for monsters.

The bright morning dimmed as the day wore on. A rain laden breeze sighed through the branches. When Kay and Gareth finally came to the edge of the forest, dark clouds were massing to the west. The sun had just dipped behind them, leaving them edged with golden fire.

Gareth saw before him, at the foot of a shallow slope, a long lake stretching away into the distance. On the nearer shore stood a grey ruin. The fluted pillars and narrow pointed arches that remained suggested that the building had once been a church, or abbey. As Gareth looked, he thought he caught a flicker of movement from the mouldering walls, but it was gone before he could be sure.

He turned to Kay. "We could spend the night there, sir. It looks like rain."

Sir Kay gave him a twisted smile. "Hoping for demons, boy? Ghosts, or some demented hermit to make a good story back at Camelot?" He shook his head. "I've been here before. They tell no tales of it."

He set his black Morial into motion down the slope. Gareth followed, disappointed. He had scarcely admitted it himself, but the ruins had seemed to promise adventure. And adventure, danger, a chance to prove himself, was what Kay needed most, so that he could be back in his proper place by the time of the Pentecost Court.

The first slow drops of rain were beginning to fall by the time Kay and Gareth reached the ruins. Most of the walls were broken down, below head height, with ivy thrusting its tendrils into the cracks between the stones. Shrubs pushed up through broken paving. The only prospect of shelter was within the central bulk of the church.

Sir Kay reined in Morial on the edge of what had once been the main approach. Gareth rode on a few paces further, until he could see through the gaping entrance arch into the cavernous space within. Everything was silent, except for a faint pattering that grew louder as the rain splashed down on stone and leaf.

Gareth dismounted and walked through the archway, glancing from side to side, feeling a prickling between his shoulder blades even though the building seemed deserted. A soft footfall just behind him made him start, but it was only Kay.

The east end of the church, furthest from where they stood, had survived better than the rest. The altar was still in place, a massive block of dressed stone. Above it the east window was bare of glass, and some of the delicate stone tracery was shattered, but the roof still covered the sanctuary and part of the choir.

"Do you want to make camp up there, sir?" Gareth asked, gesturing.

"Yes. Take the horses and –"

Gareth too had heard the sound that made him break off. It was a muffled, regular thumping, and it seemed to come from a small archway in the wall to the left, where a flight of steps led downwards.

Kay listened for a moment and then moved cautiously over to the archway. "Stay there," he said to Gareth as he started to descend.

Gareth ignored the order, as he suspected Kay knew he would, and followed him down. The dim light from the church soon died away behind them. Gareth could hear Kay's footsteps ahead of him, and his quick breathing, but he could see nothing. The rhythmic thumping was growing louder.

A change in the air told him at last that he had come to the foot of the narrow stair and stood in a more open space. Groping, his hand touched a cloaked shoulder; Kay's voice said irritably, "Damn you, boy, do you want to scare me witless?" Seconds later his hand gripped Gareth's arm and he added urgently, "Don't move from here. If we lose the stair we might never get out."

Gareth could see the sense of that. He braced himself across the opening, hands against rough stone, and listened as Kay took a few more paces in the direction of the sound.

"What's that? Who's there?" the seneschal called.

The pounding stopped. A voice, but not an echo, repeated, "Who's there?"

Gareth scarcely heard Kay's reply. The man who had spoken was his brother Gaheris.

"Kay, is that you?" he went on. "We're prisoners here. Can you open the door?"

Gareth heard Kay's footsteps again, followed by the sound of a heavy door being shaken, and then Kay's voice. "No key here. I'll go and fetch a stone to break the lock."

"Wait – take care." Gareth recognised this speaker as Sir Ector de Maris. "Have you seen Lancelot?"

"No. Should I have?"

"We were riding together," Sir Ector said. "We thought to spend the night here. But as we set foot in the abbey church a darkness fell on us, and Gaheris and I woke to find ourselves here. Where Lancelot may be, I have no idea."

"Enchantment?" said Kay. His voice was sharp with apprehension.

"It may be," said Gaheris. "Kay, go and find your rock. Get us out of here and we can look for Lancelot together."

Kay grunted an assent. Gareth heard his footsteps again, spoke his name to guide him towards the opening, and followed him back up the stairs.

"What is this?" he said. "We felt nothing. Was it a plan to trap Lancelot..?"

"Be quiet, boy," said Kay. "Stop trying to do your thinking with your tongue."

He came to the top of the steps and halted so abruptly that Gareth, hard behind him, almost cannoned into him. Over Kay's shoulder he saw what had startled him. A light had been kindled on the altar.

Not candles, but fire. Bright flames leaping from a ring of stones. And from the far end of the church, from a doorway that might once have led to a vestry, a figure appeared, and paced forward slowly to lay more twigs on the fire.

He was tall, dark-cloaked, his face hidden in the deep folds of his hood. He moved without sound. Gareth felt a tightness in his throat. Ghost, or enchanter? Or some enemy of Arthur who had laid a trap here for the king's greatest knight?

He felt Kay's hand touch his wrist and then withdraw, while Kay's attention remained focused on the dark figure.

"Gareth," the seneschal murmured, his voice no more than a faint disturbance of the air, "go and find that rock, and let them out. Quietly."

There was no time to question the startling thing that Sir Kay had just said. No time for anything but to obey. Gareth slid silently along the wall until he came to a place where it had fallen away, and picked up a stone. He straightened up, and as he turned back all thoughts of obedience were driven out of his head. Sir Kay had drawn his sword and was approaching the thing behind the altar.

Gareth almost cried out. Whatever it was, it had captured Sir Ector and Gaheris, and done something unnamed with Lancelot. If a sword could destroy it, the creature would have been destroyed already. Still hefting the rock, drawing his belt knife with the other hand, he sped up the length of the nave.

Sir Kay stood at the foot of the sanctuary steps. The cloaked figure was still, and although Gareth could not see its eyes, he fancied they were fixed on Kay.

"Are you man, or demon?" the seneschal asked. "What do you want here?"

"I could ask you that, sir knight." The creature's voice was vibrant, low-pitched, and for a second Gareth thought that he ought to recognise it.

"I am Sir Kay, High Seneschal of Britain. I came here for shelter, no more. But now I find two knights imprisoned, and a third vanished. What do you know of that?"

"More than you might think, Sir Kay. And you shall know it too, before the night is much older. If you have the courage to hear, and see."

Kay's eyes were bright and intent. "I dare look on anything you may show me."

"Then sheathe your sword. It will not avail you here."

For a moment Kay hesitated, and then slid his sword back into its scabbard.

The creature went on, "You shall have the lives of these three knights if you dare abide my testing. But think well. Sir Ector, Sir Gaheris and Sir Lancelot have all failed. Does Sir Kay dare to think that he will succeed?"

Kay hesitated again. Gareth knew well enough the self-doubt that hid behind the seneschal's irascible manner. But he knew too that there could be only one answer to the question.

"I dare to try," Kay said.

The dark figure moved forward from behind the altar until it stood over Kay. In the dying light it seemed ready to melt into the shadows. It raised a hand and beckoned. "Come."

Kay drew a harsh breath. Then, to Gareth's utter amazement, he sprang up the sanctuary steps and flung himself on the cloaked figure. He dragged at the hood, tearing it back from the hidden head. Gareth could not stop himself from crying out. No ghost or demon stood revealed there. It was Sir Lancelot.

Kay's rush had driven him back a pace or two against the altar; his hands went for Lancelot's throat. Lancelot chopped downwards across his wrists, seized his arms and bore him to the ground, but Kay somehow overbalanced him, and the two knights rolled, locked together, down the steps and on to the cracked flagstones of the choir.

Lancelot had by far the greater height and weight, but Kay fought as if madness possessed him. Whether he meant to kill Lancelot, Gareth could not tell. For a moment they writhed in a furious embrace, and then Lancelot tore himself free, and held Kay pinned on his back.

Kay's face was twisted with anguish. He spat out a helpless curse. Quite calm, Lancelot said nothing, but released him, got up and held out a hand to help Kay to his feet. Kay rolled over and buried his face in the crook of his arm.

Appalled, Gareth started towards him, but almost at once Kay pushed himself to his knees, then his feet, and stood facing Lancelot. His breath was coming in short, shallow gasps.

"You knew," said Lancelot. "How did you know?"

"If you disguise yourself, Lancelot," Kay said unsteadily, "I suggest you remove your ring."

Lancelot raised his hand and glanced at the heavy seal ring. He shrugged. "Stupid of me. I'm sorry."

"Sorry? For the stupidity?" Kay was recovering now; his voice was barbed. "Or for this whole ridiculous masquerade? Are we so short of enemies in Arthur's realm that we can waste our time playing silly games?"

Lancelot held his hands out apologetically. He wore a faint smile. "We meant to help you, Kay."

Kay's eyes narrowed. "Help me? How?"

Behind Gareth, his brother Gaheris spoke. "I knew it would never work."

Gareth glanced round. Gaheris and Ector were emerging from the archway that led to the stair, and walked towards them up the length of the church. Feeling foolish, Gareth let fall the rock he was still clutching, and sheathed his belt knife.

"We talked last night, after you made your vow," Gaheris said. "Kay, none of us want to lose you. We thought we could…" His voice died away and he could not meet Kay's eyes any longer.

"You thought you could deceive me," Kay began softly. "To make me believe I had done a great deed."

"So that you could go home," said Gaheris. He shook his head helplessly; his face was flushed with embarrassment. "Gawain told us not to do it."

"And if I had returned?" Kay said. He still spoke in the same quiet voice; Gareth would have found it less terrifying if he had been raging. "Returned and told my story in the great hall at supper, as knights do when their quests are fulfilled? What would I have done when the truth came out?"

"We would not have spoken of it," Sir Ector said.

Kay's brows lifted. More abrasively, he asked, "For how long? Until the next time you take a cup of wine too many?"

Lancelot paced slowly across the choir and stood beside his two companions. "Sir Kay, we did what we thought best," he said. "It was meant in kindness. Can you not take it so?"

"Kindness?" Kay flung the word back at him. His rage was breaking out now. "Kindness, to set my knighthood at nothing? To show the whole world that my right to sit at the Table is based on lies? Truly, Sir Lancelot, if that is your kindness, then I want none of it!" He took a deep, shuddering breath. His voice uncertain again, he spoke to Gaheris. "Did Arthur know?"

"No."

Kay's eyes closed. Gareth was afraid he might collapse, and moved hurriedly to his side. Kay turned on him; fury still coursed through him, sustaining him if nothing else would. "And you? Were you part of this? Did you bring me here so that they –"

"No!" Gareth protested, at the same time as Lancelot spoke, his voice harsh and measured.

"The boy knew nothing. At least, if you fling our good will back in our faces, let him alone."

Sir Kay took a breath as if he would reply, but said nothing. His eyes flicked from one to the other, his hawk's face wild with pain. Gareth reached out a hand to him, but he ignored it. Spinning round, without another word, he almost ran out of the ruined church.

Lancelot sighed, shaking his head. "He was ever so."

"But he's right." Gaheris sounded thoroughly miserable. "We should not…"

With nothing to add to what they might say, Gareth was making for the doorway when Lancelot called him back.

"Boy, you're welcome to share our fire tonight," he said.

Gareth could not help a little tug of longing, a little pride that he had been noticed by the great Lancelot. But he shook his head. "Thank you, sir. But I'm vowed to Sir Kay's service."

He bowed, and went out after Kay into the rain and the night.

Sir Kay had found a sheltered spot where a tree leant over the broken wall, and he was unsaddling the horses. Gareth was relieved to see that; at least the seneschal was not in such a passion that he would try riding off into this filthy night.

Gareth collected his pack without speaking, uncorded his bedding roll and stretched the canvas covering over the angle where two walls met, pinning it down with loose stones to make a rough shelter. Then, with the dry kindling he always carried on a journey and fallen branches that smoked sullenly, he managed to get a fire going.

By then Kay had finished with the horses, but still stood beside them, one hand on Morial's neck, his head and shoulders bowed. Gareth went to him and touched his arm.

"Sir?" Kay did not move. "Sir, it's all over now. Come and rest."

Kay raised his head and looked at him. If he had wept, the rain covered his tears. He was stupefied by exhaustion; he did not try to resist as Gareth guided him into the shelter. Now that there was no more for him to do, and no one but Gareth to see, he had given in. Gareth crouched beside him, eased off his sodden cloak and wrapped a dry blanket round his shoulders.

Kay shrank into the warmth it offered. "You should be with Lancelot and the others," he said.

Gareth met his eyes steadily. "If that's what you really want, sir, then give the order."

Sir Kay hesitated. Then, awkwardly, he reached out and fastened thin fingers round Gareth's wrist. "No, don't go," he murmured.

Gareth could scarcely believe the touch, or the appeal. Kay's eyes were fixed on him, a brooding, intense gaze beneath dishevelled dark hair. He had been driven out, beyond his pride and the armour of sarcasm, beyond the difference in their age and status, to the heart of his need. Only for a moment; then his courage failed him and he began to draw back, but Gareth captured his hand and clasped it between both his own.

For a while they sat in silence, except for the rain drumming on the makeshift roof, and the crackle of the fire as the wet wood took hold. Occasionally they could hear movement from the horses, or a snatch of talk from that other fireside, just visible behind the broken wall of the church.

Gareth wanted to ask what they would do in the morning, but he was not sure he could face the answer. In the end it was Kay who spoke. "You may as well sleep; I can't."

"I will, soon," Gareth promised. "But –" The memory brought a smile to his lips. "But there's something I want to ask you first." Kay's brows went up, with a glint of his old vitality. "How long have you known who I am?"

Kay looked utterly bewildered, and Gareth saw that in all the stress of what had happened afterwards, he had forgotten.

"You called me Gareth," he said. "When we saw the fire on the altar. How long have you known?"

Kay's eyes grew bright with triumph, and he was smiling a little. Their fire warmed the thin, aquiline features.

"I didn't know, not until now. But I've suspected for a long time. It was… oh, mostly it was how you talked to Gawain. And you have a look of him. None of it makes sense, unless you're his brother."

Gareth found himself pierced by a sudden delight that he could not explain. "You won't tell anyone else, sir?"

"Of course not." Kay's voice had strengthened. "Gawain already knows, I take it? None of this romantic nonsense of not recognising his own brother?"

"No," Gareth said, "but I made him promise – and the others – not to give me away. I wanted to do it like this."

Kay had grown serious again, eyeing Gareth curiously. "In God's name, boy, why? You could have walked into the court and been welcomed by everyone. Instead of which, you spend a year scrubbing the kitchen floors and putting up with Kay's sharp tongue…"

Gareth laughed. Daringly, he said, "Yes, sir, I didn't bargain for that! But if I'd just introduced myself when I came last Pentecost, then for the rest of my life I'd have been Gawain's little brother. I love Gawain, but I didn't want that."

Kay was nodding understandingly. "I think we might say that you've made your mark." The acid in his voice was back, but his eyes were dancing. "If only on the kitchen floors… You'll ask to be made knight at Pentecost?"

"Yes."

Gareth paused, looking at Kay. Even though the seneschal seemed to have revived, shaking off the leaden weight of exhaustion, Gareth knew that he had been through too much. He needed rest. But there was something Gareth wanted to ask him, and he might never have another opportunity like this one. "Sir…" he went on hesitantly.

"Yes?"

"I don't have to be knighted by Arthur, do I? I mean, another knight could do it?"

Kay looked puzzled, but replied readily. "Yes, of course. I see – you want Gawain. Or Lancelot? He thinks very highly of you, I know, and he –"

"No," Gareth interrupted. Now he had got the conversation where he wanted it, he had started to feel uncomfortable. "I don't want Lancelot to knight me. I want you."

Kay drew back from him, against the crumbling stone, staring at him. His mouth was a hard line. "That's a cruel joke, Gareth," he said. "No more than I've deserved, perhaps, but –"

"It's not a joke."

Kay went on staring at him with eyes grown bright once more, but not with triumph. He swallowed, and raised a hand to his throat. "Gareth, Lancelot is the greatest knight in the world. Your own brother is the only man who comes anywhere near him. And I –"

Gareth seized the cold, wet hands. "And you're my dear Sir Kay, who scolded me, and plagued me, and looked after me. It's what I want. Please."

Kay snatched his hands away and covered his face. "No." His voice was harsh. "Think of yourself – of your reputation – of beginning your career with the awful burden round your neck of being knighted by Sir Kay. You would be a laughing stock from here to Orkney. No."

After a moment he raised his head, looking at Gareth with a kind of weary despair. "I can't, Gareth. But I'll never forget that you asked me."

Gareth reached out, but this time did not dare to touch. He did not understand Kay, the bitterness and the wrecked life, or perhaps what he did not understand was why the others saw Kay as they did. But he realised that in what he had just asked he had been as cruel and thoughtless as the knights who, out of mistaken concern, had set Kay's knightly vows at nothing.

"I'm sorry," he said.

Kay took a breath. "I claim your promise," he said. "Ride home tomorrow. You'll need time to get ready for the Pentecost Court."

"I can't leave you, sir," Gareth protested.

"No; you must." The voice was cold, but the eyes, dark and anguished, contradicted it. "It's best. I don't want anything for you less than the best."

He turned his head away. Gareth wanted to comfort him, wanted to sit beside him again and take him in his arms and let him weep away the agony, but he was afraid that in trying he would do more damage still to this man whose self-loathing he was only just beginning to comprehend.

With an effort to stay calm, he said, "You'll always be my friend, sir."

Very slowly, Kay turned back to him. "Don't be a fool," he said, his voice growing louder, harsher. "You're young, Gareth, you have your reputation to make. You can't afford to have Kay as a friend."

Gareth felt tears stinging his eyes, closing up his throat. This calculation, this talk of reputation as something the world saw, something entirely separate from his inner self, this choosing of friends for advantage and not as his heart demanded… this was not what he had thought it meant to be a knight.

"You can't stop me, sir." He was almost shouting now. "You can't make me your enemy!"

Footsteps crunched across the broken flagstones. Sir Lancelot stepped into the circle of firelight. Rain sleeted silver across his dark cloak and dark hair, plastering it against the bony face. "What's going on?" he asked. "Kay, must you quarrel even here?"

"It's not –" Gareth began, but Kay forestalled him, springing to his feet. The blanket slipped away and he stood unprotected in the downpour. "Meddle in your own affairs, Lancelot," he said.

"It is my affair," Lancelot said austerely, "if you abuse the boy here, who has given you good service and got little thanks for it."

Gareth got to his feet and went to stand by Kay's side. The look his master gave him was fierce.

"Take him, then," he said to Lancelot. "Make of him what you will, for I've done with him."

Against the savagery and pain in his face, Gareth could find no words. He did not move, but Lancelot came to him and laid a hand on his shoulder. "Come, boy," he said.

Uncertainly, Gareth glanced at Kay, who gave him no help. Lancelot added, "You'll ride home in the morning, back to your knighting. I shall defer my vow to escort you. And let Sir Kay ride where he chooses."

At his words, Kay let out a breath, a gust of air, incredibly a sound of triumph. "I too shall ride home tomorrow, Lancelot," he said. "But not in your company."

"Forsworn?" Lancelot asked.

Kay raised his hands and slicked back streaming hair. "Call me oathbreaker, call me what it pleases you," he said. "But I know that I have performed a deed tonight that matches any of yours, Sir Lancelot, and more. I have fulfilled my vow, and I will go home."

Lancelot looked incredulous. Disapprovingly, he said, "It ill becomes me, sir, to doubt your word," and to Gareth he repeated, "Come."

For a moment Gareth could not move. Only he knew what Kay's deed had been: nothing that would bring him glory, but more valiant indeed than any other knight could claim. Renunciation: he had severed the bond with Gareth and left him free. But Gareth did not know if either of them would survive the wound.

He knew that if he stayed with Kay he would break down irrevocably, he would do and say things that Kay would not be able to bear. Choking back a sob, he gave way to the pressure of Lancelot's hand on his shoulder, and stumbled away into the pelting darkness.

Sir Kay's Quest

The music faltered into silence. Voices and laughter died. Someone cleared his throat. The eyes of all the knights and ladies of the court of Camelot were fixed on the woman who stood, calm, between the tables.

She was a slight figure, dressed in a black mantle, her silver hair braided neatly around her head. Her hands were held out towards the king, and across her forearms lay a cloak. It was of no colour and yet all colours, a rainbow shimmer shot through with silver.

"Whoever wears this cloak, my lord," she said, "will stand revealed to you in his true nature. You will see plainly all the secrets of his heart. Who will you command to wear it? Your queen? Or your good knight Sir Lancelot?"

Beside the king, Guenevere met the woman's challenging stare. She was flushed, her eyes immoderately bright. On Arthur's other side, Sir Lancelot sat and played with a few crumbs of bread on the tablecloth. Arthur looked from one to the other, disquiet growing in his face. The strange woman's lips curved into a smile.

Pushing back his chair, with a deliberately harsh noise in the breathless silence, Sir Gawain rose. "My lord, with your leave, I —"

As if his movement had released it, a babble of voices broke out around him, and by his side his brother Gareth bounded to his feet.

"I'll wear it, Uncle, willingly," he said, already moving round the table into the open space where the woman was standing.

With a faint smile, Gawain resumed his own seat. Gareth was already receiving the cloak from the woman, who looked less than pleased, and stepped backwards to avoid the swirling folds as

Gareth swung the cloak onto his shoulders and stood, a little embarrassed, for the inspection of the court.

In truth, Gawain thought, he looked no different. Gareth resembled nothing so much as a half-trained hound puppy, eager and affectionate; Gawain doubted that he had ever in his whole life had a thought he wanted to conceal. The tension of the onlookers was beginning to dissolve in laughter and scattered applause.

Then a voice spoke. "Oh, virtuous Gareth…"

The tones were low, but meant to carry. Gareth's head jerked round; he was thrown off balance, uncertain how he should reply. Gawain also turned.

The speaker was Sir Kay, a place or two down the table. He leant forward a little, his aquiline features alive with some feeling Gawain could not define.

"How fortunate you are," he went on silkily, "to abide the test with so little to show for it. One might almost think the cloak has no such power."

Gareth shrugged out of the cloak, and returned it to the woman's waiting hands. Her gaze was venom, aimed at Sir Kay.

"If you think so, sir," she said to him, "then try it for yourself."

A chorus of voices echoed her; there were plenty of people who would be pleased to see Kay put to the test, and who would have willingly predicted the result. Kay's acerbic tongue had won him few friends.

Gawain watched thoughtfully, frowning. Kay had half risen; he had gone quite white, and had lifted a hand to his throat, as if he found it hard to breathe. He was, plainly, terrified. Gawain did not understand. Whatever Kay might be, he was not stupid; he must have known his challenge would have brought this counter-challenge down on him.

The woman took a step towards him and held out the cloak. "Sir? If you please?"

Kay sank back into his seat. "No," he said.

Like a whiplash the woman turned back to the king. "My lord – your… follower has cast doubt on my truth. I demand the right to prove it to you!"

Silence fell again as the king weighed her words, looking from her to Kay. Then he said, "Kay, come and stand here, before us."

Gawain realised that for a brief time, Arthur had been at a loss, but now strength was back in the measured voice. Slowly, with clear reluctance, Kay left his seat. He was a spare, elegant man, and now he had himself in hand again, pride in his carriage and the way he held his head, but Gawain could feel the tension singing out of him.

"Put on the cloak," the king said.

"My lord, I will not."

The blunt refusal brought an outbreak of murmuring, and someone, lower down the table said, audibly, "Coward." Kay's head went up, and his mouth tightened.

"You disobey me?" the king inquired gently.

"I refuse to take part in this foolishness." Kay's tones were scathing. "I suggest, madam, that if you wish to show us proof, you wear the cloak yourself."

Though he was not its target, Gawain almost felt himself flinching at the concentration of evil will that was hurled at Kay. It seemed as if the woman's power could shrivel him to dust; then, in an instant, it was gone, as she herself was, and the cloak with her, vanished from the midst of the hall with no one to be certain of the manner of her going.

Uproar. A few words that passed between Sir Kay and the king were drowned in the clamour. Sir Kay bowed formally and was turning away when one voice was lifted above all the others.

"Traitor!"

Gawain stiffened. The voice belonged to his brother, Sir Agravaine, who was sitting at the other side of the hall, too far away to be silenced. He was getting to his feet as the noise once more died away and he could make himself heard.

"My lord, there is treachery here!"

Gawain sighed. Agravaine had never learnt when to leave well enough alone.

"The woman could have done you great service," he continued. "The cloak would have shown you which of your knights you can trust. Yet now it is gone. And why was Sir Kay so unwilling to wear it that he disobeyed your direct command?"

Kay had been returning to his seat, but now he stopped and faced Agravaine.

"Forgive me; I must be going deaf," he said, "since I failed to hear your offer to wear the cloak."

The barbed words had Agravaine blustering; Gawain hid a smile. But the accusation was not so easily turned aside. Others had taken up the cry of treachery; at last, the king raised his hand for silence.

"Sir Kay," he said, "is there anything you want to say to me?"

"Not here, my lord." He swung round at a muttered jibe behind him. "But this I will say. With your leave, I will go from here, and I will seek out this enchantress with her cloak. And if it is good, I will bring it to you, but if it is evil, I will destroy it. More than that – when I find it, I will wear it, and you shall see if I carry any treason in my heart."

In a vast silence, he stalked out of the hall.

Gawain tapped on the door. Inside he could hear faint movements, but no command to enter. When a second tap brought the same result, he swung the door open and stepped inside uninvited. At first Kay seemed not to realise he was there. He had flung a pair of saddlebags down on the bed, and he was packing, with quick, nervous, uncoordinated movements. When he saw Gawain, he stopped.

"What do you want?"

"A word with you," Gawain said agreeably.

He closed the door and remained standing by it. Kay went on with his packing.

"Was this really necessary?" Gawain asked.

"After Agravaine had accused me of treason?" Kay's voice was biting. "No, I suppose I could have challenged him, and let him grind me into the floor of the tilting ground tomorrow. I prefer this way. I'm sorry if Agravaine is disappointed."

Gawain shrugged, dismissing Agravaine. "You certainly walked into trouble, didn't you?" he said. "Why?"

Kay paused in what he was doing and looked at him, dark eyes snapping. "Why does Kay do anything?" he demanded. "Just a natural tendency to be disagreeable!"

Gawain smiled at him. "You wouldn't have been creating a diversion, would you?" he asked. "A diversion we badly needed – before the challenge could lie where it could not be answered?"

Before Gawain had finished speaking Kay had turned away and began jerking roughly at the saddlebag straps. After a moment, he asked, "Did the king send you?"

"No. But he knows I'm here."

"Why? What do you want with me?"

Gawain hesitated. He had expected hostility, but not this raw pain, so that every word was like searching an open wound. At last he said quietly, "I want to come with you, if you'll have me."

At that, Kay straightened up and faced him, staring. "Why?" he asked bitterly. "Does Arthur want a spy? Or does he think I need someone to hold my hand?"

"No," Gawain replied. "But you might need a witness." When Kay said nothing, he went on: "You must not bring the cloak back into the court, you know that." Kay made an impatient gesture, but gave no other reply. "Then you will either look for it and fail and return empty-handed, or find it, wear it and then destroy it, and return empty-handed –"

"And no one will believe the story I tell," Kay finished for him. "But they will believe Sir Gawain, the courteous, the flower of knighthood, the –"

"I want to help," Gawain interrupted.

For a moment Kay went on staring at him. His hands were clenched. Gawain realised that for whatever reason, this man was very close to breaking.

"Please," Gawain said.

Kay looked away. His incisive voice was suddenly blurred. "You may do as you please," he said. "I can't stop you. And if you tire of my company, you can always leave me and come home."

Gawain relaxed, once more able to smile. "Well, yes," he said. "I can always do that."

Riding with Sir Kay, Gawain found, was rather like picking blackberries. The fruit is sweet, but sooner or later, however careful you might be, you are going to get scratched. Gawain no longer thought of his companion's ill humour as a natural tendency to be disagreeable; there was some deep-rooted cause, but what that might be, Gawain could not imagine. But he had a clearer idea of why Kay had not wanted to wear the cloak in the presence of all the court.

For several days they rode aimlessly. There had never been any hope of following the enchantress; she had her own ways of travelling. But Gawain had learnt long before that if a deep need drives you to your destination you will find it in the end. And Kay was a man driven.

One evening, in that twilight when colours fade and shapes blur into the background, a deceptive light that was harder than true darkness, they found their way into a narrow valley. A stream slid silent over flat stones. Furze and hazel brakes lined the slopes. And at the head of the valley they came to a turf-covered mound, with a dolmen arch in its side.

They reined in and looked at each other.

"I don't like it," Kay said.

"I don't suppose it was put here for our approval," Gawain returned mildly.

He slid from his horse and twisted the reins around a nearby branch. Slipping a little on loose stones underfoot, he made his way towards the mound until he stood under the ash-grey lintel. Kay said, "Don't. Come away."

Gawain glanced back at him. He was still mounted, with his hand at the fastening of his cloak, that familiar gesture, as if he found it difficult to breathe. Turning from him, Gawain rested both hands on the stone uprights and looked into the mound. A narrow passage led straight ahead, walls of roughly dressed stone soon becoming lost in darkness.

Behind him he heard footfalls coming closer, and then Kay's voice at his shoulder.

"Gawain. It's... evil. Come away."

"We're looking for evil, or had you forgotten?"

"You think... here?"

Gawain stepped back from the entrance. It was a long time since he had felt such a profound sense of evil, as if it was coiling down the passage-way, dark and sticky, to spatter itself all over him. Calmly, he said, "If not the cloak, then something else, just as powerful."

Kay had shrunk back, shuddering, but as Gawain watched he straightened up and said, "Then stand aside. This is for me to do. Wait here, and if I don't come out, you can ride home and tell your tale."

He put a hand on the hilt of his sword, and stepped forward under the arch. Gawain let him go, and then closed in behind him.

"You don't get rid of me that easily," he murmured. Like Kay, he loosened his sword in its sheath, but he did not think that swords would be much use against anything they might find in the mound.

The passage ran straight on. Soon the dim light from the entrance died away behind them and they moved on into darkness, groping their way forward. Gawain could hear nothing but their soft footsteps and Kay's uneven breathing, until gradually he began to realise that he could see Kay's figure ahead of him, outlined against a faint, pale light. Then they were stepping through another archway, into a circular, domed chamber.

Gawain stood still in amazement. They were in a chapel, with steps leading up to the sanctuary, an altar covered with a white cloth and an embroidered frontal, a sanctuary lamp burning. There was a faint smell of incense. No one else was there, but it was not deserted; rather it seemed as if the priest had just left, and might return at any moment. Gawain might have relaxed, if he could have shaken off that overwhelming sense of evil.

On the altar there stood something that might have been a chalice, hidden from their sight by the white linen cloth placed over it. From beneath the cloth, a pure, pearly light welled out, spilling into every crevice of the chapel. At Gawain's side, Kay breathed out, "Beautiful…"

He was gazing, rapt, at the altar. His habitual sardonic expression had dissolved away; he looked oddly defenceless. He said, "I want to –"

He took a step forward and stopped himself.

Gawain felt his heart wrenched. "Go on," he said softly. "If it is truly what it seems to be, then it is here for you. But – Kay, be careful."

Kay seemed not to have heard the last warning. He was still gazing at the altar, torn apart by his terror and longing.

"I can't," he said. "Gawain, I can't. I'm not –" He pressed a hand to his lips. "I can't," he repeated. "Gawain, you might be worthy, but I – oh, no, no."

Gently Gawain took his arm and drew him forward as far as the sanctuary steps, where they knelt together. What Kay's prayer might be, Gawain never knew; for himself he prayed for guidance, and for help, for all his senses were still screaming danger.

At length, with a long sigh, Kay crossed himself, rose, and took a step towards the altar. His hands shaking, he lifted the cloth. For a long moment he stared at what he saw. From where he still knelt, Gawain could not see it, but he saw the light redden, so that Kay's hands looked as if they were washed in blood. He heard the rasping sound in Kay's throat, as if he tried to cry out and could not, saw him start back with his hands over his face, to fall backwards from the sanctuary steps and crash to the stone floor of the chapel.

Instantly, the light went out. But before darkness clamped down, Gawain had also seen the death's head on the altar, the jaw dropped in an eternal rictus, worms slithering, pullulating, in the empty eye sockets, and smelt fetid air wafting from the charnel house. From the darkness came a faint, dry snickering.

Gawain crawled across the floor of the chapel until he found Kay's body and made sure that he was still breathing. Carefully he raised Kay's head, eased it on to his lap, and examined it, with a fingertip touch, for any hurt.

There was nothing, no bleeding wound at least, though in the darkness Gawain could be sure of nothing else. He was relieved when, not long after, Kay gave a quick, convulsive movement and clutched at him.

"Gawain?"

"Yes."

"Gawain, I can't see." Terror pulsed in his voice.

Gently, Gawain slid an arm around him and helped him to sit up. "Don't worry, you're not blind," he said. "It's dark, that's all."

Kay was still clinging to him. "Merciful God, where are we?"

"Still in the mound. You were unconscious for a few minutes, no more."

"Gawain, did you see?" Kay's voice was shaking. "That – thing – Is it…?"

"Gone, I think," Gawain reassured him. "Are you hurt? Can you walk? I think we should try to get out of here."

"Are we trapped?" Kay choked on a sob of panic. Gawain could feel his body racked by his struggles for self-mastery. "Oh, God, Gawain," he broke out with an echo of his old bitterness, "they were right when they called me a coward. If you were not here, I think I should lose my reason."

Gawain found himself smiling in the darkness. "Then they can call me coward too," he said, "for I'm certain if you were not here, I should lose mine. Can you stand? Come, then."

He helped Kay to his feet and supported him. Even in the darkness, he had not lost all sense of direction; he could feel the faint movement of cooler air against his face. But as he moved towards the entrance, light began to grow once more. It was all around them, as if it was seeping out of the stones. They halted, and turned.

Where the altar had been, at the top of the steps, was a lady, seated on a carved and gilded chair. Hands like claws curved round the chair's arms. She wore the rainbow cloak, its shimmering folds spilling around her. In it, she was a vision of resplendent evil. She was, and yet was not, the woman who had brought the cloak to Camelot. Gawain knew her, but it was Kay who named her. "Morgan le Fay," he said. "I should have known."

Morgan's gaze flicked over Gawain and then withdrew to focus again on Kay.

"Sir Kay." She returned his acknowledgment. "You have inconvenienced me. Which is to your credit. Many better men than you have inconvenienced me and not lived to boast of it."

"You overwhelm me, madam." That was the old Kay, keenly sarcastic, resurfacing out of the fear and revulsion. "Since we talk of inconvenience, what about the game you have played with us here?"

"Game? You have scarcely cause for complaint, when you walk uninvited into one of my secret places. But since you are here –" Her glance went back to Gawain; she smiled, which encouraged him not at all. "Since you are here, tell me what I can do for you."

Gawain suspected that she knew already, but she waited with apparent patience while Kay repeated the story of the pledge he had made in the hall at Camelot. "I have sworn to find the cloak, to wear it, and to destroy it," he ended.

"Wear it? Certainly," Morgan said. "As for destroying it, you are welcome to try." She stood and slipped off the cloak. Without it, she seemed diminished: not beautiful, not powerful, a woman you would pass without a second glance. She held out the cloak to Kay.

He advanced hesitantly to the foot of the steps, took the cloak, and stood for a moment, crushing the rainbow fabric together in his hands. Morgan's smile grew cruel as she reseated herself.

"Afraid, Sir Kay? Afraid of what Gawain will see in you?"

Kay turned to Gawain, desperation and pleading in his eyes. Gawain came to his side. "Give it to me," he said. "I'll wear it first."

With misgivings he did not let himself think about, he took the cloak and draped it over his shoulders. As Kay gazed at him, Gawain saw his face change, recalling his softened look as he stood before the radiant light on the altar. He whispered, "No difference at all, Gawain."

Gawain swallowed tears in his throat. Stepping forward, he took off the cloak; Kay flinched away from him. "You're not afraid of me, are you?" Gawain said softly.

He folded the cloak around his friend. He could feel Kay's trembling, but he stood erect, head up, and his gaze never left Gawain's.

His appearance did not change. But it was as though Gawain's perceptions had shifted, so that he could see and understand so much that Kay had striven to hide. First, and most deeply rooted, a devotion to Arthur that Gawain had never guessed at. The haunting fear that nothing of what he felt could be returned. The defences he had built with sharp tongue and disdainful manner, and the spirit battering itself to destruction against the walls he himself had raised.

Gawain stepped forward, pulled off the cloak and tossed it to lie in a shimmering heap at Morgan's feet, and drew Kay into his embrace.

"It's over," he said. "It's over, and you have won."

Briefly, Kay clung to him. Morgan had risen to her feet again. She looked murderous; Gawain could well understand why. Kay had thwarted her in her attempt to use the cloak to break the fellowship of the Round Table, and now it had been worthless even as the instrument of her revenge. She flung out a hand towards it, as if casting something down among the folds.

As she did so, the fabric lost its shape; a ripple passed through it; it began to flow, and cascaded down the steps as a stream of water, to be lost as it soaked through the cracks between the paving stones. At the same moment, the light began to die.

"You may have won," Morgan said, "but you will not live to enjoy it."

She began to laugh. Across the sound of her laughter came a faint rasping sound, and a fine trickle of soil began to fall from the chapel roof. Gawain understood. He thrust Kay towards the entrance as the rasping sound grew louder, and Morgan's laughter was drowned in the roar of earth and stone as the roof fell in behind them.

They struggled along the passage, the ground shifting under their feet, the walls pressing in. The air was filled with the noise of grinding stone. Gawain could see the outline of the arch leading to the open air, but it seemed to waver, like a shape seen under water. Then something sharp struck him on the head, and he saw nothing more.

Gawain opened his eyes on glimmering light and darkness. The air was cool. He lay on grass, wrapped in a blanket. As his senses returned, he could make out the moon riding high above trees, cloud drifting across its face. Struggling, he raised himself on one elbow and looked around him.

Not far away, a fire was burning. Their packs were heaped up beside it, and beyond it their horses cropped the grass. There was no sign of the mound, only, where it had stood, an irregular hummock covered with turf; rough, lichen-covered stones jutted out from it here and there. Gawain sighed.

A light footfall told him of Kay's approach. He came up from the stream, carrying their waterskins. When he saw Gawain was awake, he gave him a shy, flickering smile, and then knelt to feed the fire.

"You brought me out of there," Gawain said.

Kay turned sharply towards him. "How could I go back to Camelot without you?" he asked abrasively. "Who would believe me then?"

"Kay, don't," Gawain said. "Not with me. Not now."

Kay held his eyes for a few seconds longer, and then bowed his head. "Forgive me," he said.

"Forgive you? I want to thank you. Without you, I would be dead. That's a story I'll be glad to tell in Camelot."

Kay's head jerked up. "No," he said.

Gawain felt exasperation overwhelm him, and at the same time he wanted to laugh, or weep. He found that he was becoming very fond of this proud, difficult, deeply unhappy man.

"Oh, very well," he said. "Quarrel with me if you want to. But I shall tell the story all the same."

Kay's hand went to his throat. "Not... the cloak... not what you saw then," he whispered. "Please."

"No, not that," Gawain agreed.

Kay came to sit beside him, and offered him one of the waterskins. "Arthur and I were brought up as brothers," he said. "Until I was sixteen, I thought he was my brother. They'll tell you now I treated him as my servant, but that isn't true. They even say that when he drew the sword out of the stone I tried to pretend that it was I who had done it. That's a lie that will dog me beyond the grave. We were brothers. And then he was the king." He sighed, and covered his eyes with one hand. "At first, it seemed as if nothing would change. Not everyone was prepared to accept him – your father among them, Gawain – and I fought at his side. He needed me."

"And no one called you coward," Gawain said.

"It was easy then. There was something worth dying for. But now..." He shook his head helplessly. "I was wrong. He was the king. Things had to change. Afterwards, there were others. There had to be. The queen, of course. And Lancelot, and you, and your brothers. How could I let Arthur think that I was making any claim on him? How could I tell him..?"

As he spoke the last words he was struggling to control his voice, and at last he lost the battle, fighting instead the wrenching sobs that broke out of him in spite of all he could do. Gawain reached out and put a hand on his shoulder.

"I would rather let them hate me –" Kay gasped out, and could not speak any more, as at last, under Gawain's touch, he could give way, and allow himself to weep.

Gawain and Kay paused at the foot of the stairs that led up to the great hall at Camelot. Light, and music, and laughter spilled from the open doors, but they stood in shadow. The last few days, the slow, quiet return home, had been precious to both of them, but now they were over. Gawain touched Kay's arm. "Ready?" he asked.

Kay, tense but controlled, nodded. They had begun to mount the stairs when a voice called, "Gawain!"

Gawain swung round; it was Agravaine. He strode up to them and stood looking from one to the other. "No cloak," he said at last.

"No," Gawain agreed. "The cloak is destroyed. As anyone could see, it was evil. But Kay wore it, in my presence, and I saw no dishonour in him. He also saved my life, if you count that of any value."

He did not look at Kay, but he was aware of him at his side, and felt his friend's struggle to bite back a scathing remark as if it were his own. Instead, Gawain watched Agravaine, and saw bewilderment give way to a knowing grin.

"Well, Gawain," he said, clapping his brother on the shoulder, "tell the tale that way if it makes you happy. Just don't expect anyone else to believe it."

He turned away and went swiftly up the steps.

Kay's hand was on his sword hilt. "He called you a liar!"

Gawain shrugged ruefully. "That's Agravaine. Take no notice. I can't very well challenge my own brother, can I? Let's get on."

But as he moved to follow Agravaine up the stairs, Kay caught his arm and held him back. "Gawain – Gawain, you can't be my friend here. Not without destroying yourself. And I won't accept that." He smiled, but already his smile had its old edge of bitterness. "You see, none of what we did together is going to make any difference at all."

He turned away, his head and shoulders bowed under the burden he had chosen for himself. Gawain spoke his name, but Kay gave no sign that he had heard. He climbed slowly, painfully, towards the lights and the laughter.

Gawain hesitated, watching him, until his dark figure showed as a silhouette against the open doorway. Suddenly he spoke aloud.

"No!" He snapped into motion again, and began to mount the stairs, quickly, almost running, to catch Kay, so that they could enter the hall side by side.

A Gift for King Arthur

Sir Gawain of Orkney never knew who first thought of the contest, though his brother Gaheris voiced it. On the last day of the year, the mid-day meal was almost over in the great hall at Carlisle. Queen Guenevere and her ladies had already withdrawn, along with the guests. Arthur still remained, with his knights around him.

The talk, light-hearted at first, was of New Year's gifts. Then Gaheris got to his feet, embarrassed in the midst of laughter, as if he was an unwilling spokesman.

"My lord Arthur," he said, "let us present our gifts to you tomorrow, and then choose the one that pleases you best."

Arthur looked surprised; a slight frown touched his face. "Have you a reward in mind?"

"No!" Gaheris reddened; he was honest, Gawain knew, if inclined to speak first and think afterwards. "Only the honour of your choice, my lord."

Gawain looked down into his wine cup. He had a gift for the king, which he meant to offer privately; he had no stomach for this sort of contest. Briefly he wished that Lancelot was at court. He would not approve, and their combined influence might have stopped it. As it was, Gawain could foresee trouble. Not everyone would accept the king's choice; with everyone restless in the middle of winter, quarrels could well lead to fighting.

Meanwhile, King Arthur had risen to his feet. "Very well," he said. "If you wish you may present your gifts to me here, after chapel tomorrow. But let it be a New Year's game, no more. I shall think no dishonour of anyone who does not take part."

He glanced down at Gawain as he said the last words, and then turned and went out through his private door.

A babble of conversation broke out. Gawain held aloof, sipping the last of his wine. Some of the knights had already begun to leave, almost sweeping aside Sir Kay the seneschal, who had come in with the servants to supervise the clearing of the tables. Kay had not eaten with the others; he gave the departing knights a look of surprise and disapproval, and strode down the hall towards Gawain.

"What's all this?" he asked. "They're like bees with the hive tipped over."

Gawain half smiled. Kay had caught well the buzz and ferment. He explained about the contest to find the gift that would please Arthur most.

"Will you take part, Kay?" Sir Lamorak asked, from further down the table.

Kay sniffed disdainfully. "I've no time to waste on such nonsense."

"Sir Kay gives nothing but insults."

Gawain stiffened. The speaker was his brother Agravaine, leaning towards Kay with a slack, insolent grin on his face. Even at mid-day, Agravaine had already drunk more than enough.

Somebody laughed. Everyone within earshot was listening.

"It's hard," Kay said, "to give you anything else, Agravaine."

"But I shall bring a gift to honour the king. Kay thinks himself too high to do the same."

Agravaine offered the comment to the rest of the table. There were murmurs of agreement.

"Kay, you presume on your position as seneschal," Sir Bors said, moralising. "Remember that no virtue of yours set you there. As Arthur's foster-brother –"

"That is not for you to speak of," Kay snapped.

"Or dare you not join the contest," Lamorak said, with a needle thrust of malice, "in case Arthur scorns your gift?"

Kay's pale features were flushed; his fiery temper, always too close to the surface, was roused now.

"Kay, don't," Gawain said softly.

Kay ignored him. "I have no need to contest for Arthur's favour." The defensive note in his voice was too clear; everyone could hear that he did not believe what he said.

Agravaine sniggered. "Too mean to buy a gift," he said, gulping his wine, "and too cowardly to win one."

Kay stepped forward; fury flared in his hawk's face. Gawain grasped his arm, but Kay shook him off. Aqravaine had drawn his belt knife, and was twirling it so that the point glittered. Kay tensed.

"This is no place for a brawl," Gawain said, looking from one to the other.

Without replying, Kay spun round and stalked off, out of the main doors. Agravaine's raucous laughter followed him.

In the courtyard, those knights who felt they did not have a worthy gift were calling for their horses to be saddled. Among them, Gawain saw Kay.

"Kay, you're surely not going to be caught up in this absurdity? Pay no attention to what they say. Everyone knows that –"

As he began to speak, Kay drew himself up. His mouth was tight, his eyes blazing. "I shall ride from here," he said, "and take what adventure it pleases God to grant me. It may be that I shall find a gift for the king. I do not need your sympathy, Sir Gawain, nor your advice."

The words were spat out, but Gawain could not find it in his heart to take offence. "I'm sorry," he said.

Kay ignored him. Just then the groom brought up his horse; he mounted and rode out of the gates without another word.

Gawain watched him go, disquiet growing within him. After a few minutes he called a groom and gave orders to have his own horse saddled.

Kay had taken the south road, but by the time Gawain was ready to follow, he was out of sight. That suited Gawain well. He would not dishonour Kay by suggesting that he might need help, unless there was no other choice.

He had not been riding for long before he began to catch glimpses of Kay ahead of him as the road wound back and forth. Gawain kept his distance, trusting to clumps of gorse and hazel brakes to screen him.

He lost sight of Kay again as the road looped around a jutting spur of rock, and as he approached it he heard the sound of voices. He reined in, dismounted, and edged forward on foot.

An unknown voice was speaking; the words turned Gawain's heart cold. "You seek a gift for King Arthur?"

"How do you know that?" Kay's voice, sharp and suspicious.

Soft laughter.

Gawain reached the spur of rock and peered round it. A few yards ahead Kay, still mounted, was speaking to a young man, dressed as a huntsman or forester, who sat on the bank at the side of the road. He was dark and boldly handsome, a tall, well-muscled body sprawling now at his ease, looking up at Kay with laughter on his lips.

Beyond him was a stand of trees, and beyond that, out of sight but well known to Gawain, was Tarn Wathelyn. This was an evil place. Gawain would trust nothing and no one that harboured anywhere near the tarn. He pressed himself against the rock, and put his hand on the hilt of his sword.

"Suppose I could show you a gift?" the young man said.

"What gift?"

"Something no king in the world has in his possession. Not even Arthur."

"And what must I give for it?"

Kay sounded impatient. Gawain felt almost like smiling. There was evil here, he knew, but Kay's quick temper might save him where caution would not.

"That I will not tell you... yet," the young man said. He smiled, all easy confidence, stretching like a great cat. "Come and see, if you dare. Or is Sir Kay a coward as all men say?"

The old taunt would inflame Kay, no doubt. He dismounted swiftly, and twisted his horse's reins around the branch of one of the trees. "Show me," he said.

The young man rose and beckoned, and seconds later both of them had vanished from Gawain's sight through the trees.

Gawain felt danger pricking him like a thousand spear points. He thought that even here he could breathe the miasma that hung around the tarn. And as the young man turned – had that been a ribbon of waterweed in his hair? Had Kay not seen it? Could he possibly be so unwary that he did not know what he was risking? Or – and Gawain's heart tore at the thought – was he so desperately unhappy that he did not care?

Cautiously, as silently as he could, Gawain slid through the trees and began tracking Kay down the slope towards the tarn. As he drew closer, his feet began to sink into the uneven turf. Behind him, his footprints filled with water.

Mist rose from the surface of the tarn. Around it, dark evergreens huddled close to the water, and beyond was a black wall, the edge of Inglewood. The short winter day was dying into dusk.

In the mist and twilight, Gawain had lost sight of Kay's guide, though he could still make out Kay himself, picking his way around clumps of sedge and patches of bog towards the shore of the tarn. He moved quickly, with a poised wariness.

Then, in the bushes, Gawain saw movement. Kay stopped; he must have seen it too. A shape gathered itself out of darkness and leapt into plain view. A horse. A magnificent black stallion, tossing its head and pawing restively at the squelchy ground.

Gawain froze. Did Kay not recognise the thing he had followed, the kelpie that could take the shape of man or horse, and was a demon in both? Then as he caught a glimpse of Kay's face, set with sick fear and determination, Gawain saw that he understood very well. If he could tame the kelpie, subdue it and ride it back to Arthur's court, would that not be the most marvellous gift that a king ever received?

The creature circled Kay, neck extended. Kay sprang for the mane, grasped it and pulled himself on to the stallion's back. It reared, pawing the air, as if it could throw him off. But Kay was a fine horseman; he kept his seat. Beneath him the kelpie bunched itself, powerful muscles rippling, and took off straight for the tarn.

All Gawain's instincts screamed at him to follow. Instead, he ran back to his own horse, and pulled off the bridle. Taking his belt knife, he scratched on the gilded leather the sign of the cross.

When he reached the shore of the tarn again, Kay and the kelpie had disappeared. Gawain paused, panting, shedding his cloak and dragging off his riding boots as he listened. Ripples rolled out of the gathering darkness and broke at his feet. He could hear sounds as if something large rolled and wallowed in the water.

He swam out into a wall of mist, the bridle looped over one arm. There was nothing to guide him except for the thrashing noise ahead and suddenly a high-pitched whinnying cry: half horse, half man, and wholly savage.

Then Gawain broke out of the mist and saw it, the head and forelegs out of the water, an impossible pose, a demi-horse of heraldry, sable on argent. The hooves lashed down. Kay no longer rode it; he clung to the mane as the kelpie tried to shake him off and overwhelm him in the surging water. His face was white, his black hair plastered over it. Blood sluiced from a cut on his temple. When he saw Gawain he gasped out his name; it could have been a plea, or a curse.

Gawain threw the bridle over the kelpie's head, struggling to pull the headstall into place. The creature convulsed and brought its head round, jaws snapping, a pulse driving through its whole body. Kay lost his grip and fell back into the water. He was floundering helplessly, exhausted, perhaps injured, and barely able to keep himself afloat.

A red eye, rolling madly. Foam on the kelpie's lips. Its head thrashed back and forth as it fought to escape. The straps tore at Gawain's hands. He could have forced the bit home, but he could hear Kay gasping and choking behind him. He let go. The kelpie tossed itself free, and plunged for the depths. The water rose in a single great surge, and was still. Gawain grabbed Kay as he sank, and began towing him back to the shore.

On New Year's Day, King Arthur sat in his high seat, in the great hall at Carlisle, and received the gifts his knights brought to him. Sir Gawain watched him, rather than the gift giving, and thought he saw on his face a look of faint distaste.

The gifts piled up. Rich garments, in fur and velvet and embroidery. Finely crafted weapons. Leather worked with jewels and gold into scabbards and belts and horse trappings. The prizes of the hunt. Gaheris, more imaginative than most, had tracked down a notorious local bandit, and presented him in chains. Arthur gave gracious thanks for everything, and let no hint of his preference show.

Kay stood apart at one side of the hall. He moved stiffly, as if he could not use his left arm; Gawain had seen the bruising the day before, where the thrashing hooves had struck down. He went across to him.

As he approached, Kay gave him a flickering glance, and looked away. The cut on his head had been dressed, his hair feathered over it. He was subdued, all his fire quenched.

"You look ill," Gawain said. "You should be in bed."

Kay shook his head. In a low voice, he said, "I told my lord Arthur everything."

"Why?"

Gawain was genuinely surprised. There was nothing exactly dishonourable about Kay's failure, but he had thought that Kay would want it decently forgotten.

Kay glanced at him again. Colour was staining his cheekbones, crudely blotching his white face. Now his voice was so quiet Gawain had to lean close to hear him. "I wished to honour you. It's all the thanks I can give."

Gawain put a hand on his shoulder. "Unnecessary."

In the body of the hall, the gift giving was over; it was time for Arthur to make his choice. Gawain had expected the king to look annoyed, or embarrassed, for clearly he had not wanted the contest in the first place. Instead, he was smiling faintly. He walked across the hall until he stood beside Kay and Gawain.

"I received two gifts," he said, "that cannot be shown here." A puzzled silence fell. Even Gawain was not sure what the king meant. "The first was a story," Arthur went on. "Told out of a generous spirit, to win honour for another." Kay had averted his face; Gawain could see his hands tightly clenched. "The second gift," the king said, "was my brother Kay's life. There are few things I value more."

Arthur drew Kay into a brief embrace, and then, releasing him but keeping an arm around his shoulders, held out his free hand to Gawain.

"Though you did not enter this contest, Sir Gawain," he said, "yet you have won it."

Gawain took the king's hand. He could see that all Kay's tension had suddenly dissolved; his eyes were brilliant. Gawain found himself smiling. Behind him, he could hear breaking out the wondering murmurs of the other knights.

King Arthur's Ransom

Sir Gareth of Orkney eased open crusted eyelids. His vision swam. He lay prone; beneath his hands he could feel moss, and the creeping foliage of the forest floor. His mouth was dry, and his head throbbed painfully.

That morning Gareth had left Camelot with King Arthur and a group of the other knights, nothing more urgent on their minds than a day's hawking. As the sun began to go down, they turned for home. Their road led through an arm of the forest. Gareth remembered passing under the branches of the outermost trees. Ahead of him, someone was singing. And then nothing, unless there might have been, glimpsed in the depths of the hazel brakes, a swirl of glittering darkness.

Blinking to clear his vision, Gareth made out the edge of the stream that ran beside the forest ride, and dragged himself towards it until he could reach down into the water. He splashed his face, rubbing the icy liquid over his eyes and forehead, and scooped it up in one hand so that he could drink.

At length, breathing hard, he sat up. Among the tall grasses and clumps of bracken, the other knights were rousing as he was, or still lay inert. Horses trampled restlessly at the edge of the ride. A hawk, its jesses tangled in a branch, bated repeatedly.

Not until Gareth stumbled to his feet and began to gather his friends together for the journey home did he realise that the king and Sir Lancelot had vanished.

It was dark by the time the knights returned to Camelot. At dawn the next day, Sir Kay the Seneschal sent out search parties. Gareth led one of them. All day they quartered the woods and fields to the north of the city, and returned empty-handed at sunset.

As they rode through the gates of the citadel, grooms came out to lead away their horses. Across the courtyard, Sir Kay was talking with men from one of the other search parties. He broke off when he saw Gareth, dismissed the men, and beckoned him over.

"Well?"

"I'm sorry – nothing. I'll go out again tomorrow."

Sir Kay shook his head irritably. He was a small man, all tightly coiled tension at the best of times; now Gareth thought he could almost see sparks flying off him.

"What use?" His mouth tightened. "Twenty-four hours… Arthur could be anywhere. No, we must –"

He broke off as the bell in the gatehouse sounded and guards began to pull the gates open again. Sir Lancelot rode through, alone. Kay bit back an exclamation and strode across to him, reaching up to grip his horse's bridle.

The words sharp as arrows, he asked, "Where is Arthur?"

"Not here." Lancelot always looked grave, but there was a deathly weariness in his face now that frightened Gareth.

"I can see that." Kay sounded exasperated and more, his quick temper barely under control. "Tell me what you know."

Lancelot dismounted. "It's fitting I speak first with the queen," he said.

"Sir Lancelot," Kay said, "If I don't have your information, how can I organise the search?" He bowed, a mocking parody of courtesy. "But five minutes of your time, noble sir, and then you may go to the queen – or the devil, for all I care."

He set off across the courtyard, not looking to see if Lancelot would follow.

Lancelot shrugged, and glanced at Gareth. "Come, then," he said. "If Kay insists, you may as well hear it too."

Kay led the way to his workroom, up the stairs from the castle kitchens. He seated himself behind his huge work table and motioned Lancelot and Gareth to chairs in the window alcove.

Lancelot seemed too restless to sit. "Gareth has told you how sleep overcame us in the forest?" he said. Kay nodded impatiently. "I woke in a prison cell," Lancelot went on. Now he told the story to Gareth, as if Kay was not in the room. "Alone. And soon I was taken to the lord of the castle." His mouth curled contemptuously. "We had met before. His name is Valerin, and he styles himself King of the Tangled Wood. Though sorcerer, I think, would be a fitter name than king. Once I fought with him and defeated him, when he dared claim rights over Queen Guenevere."

"And did he challenge you again?" Gareth asked.

Lancelot shook his head. "He set me against his champion, that he calls the Golden Knight. A man all in golden armour. I never saw his face. For all I know he is some sorcerous creature, not a man at all."

"And when you defeated him..?" Gareth asked eagerly.

Lancelot looked down at his hands. His face, that rarely showed emotion, had reddened. "I lost the fight," he admitted.

Sir Kay let out a short crack of laughter. "Welcome to the human race, Lancelot."

Sir Lancelot ignored him. To Gareth, he went on, "King Arthur is Valerin's prisoner too. Valerin spared my life and sent me with a demand for Arthur's ransom. I left his castle, and found myself back in the forest, not an hour's ride from here."

"And the ransom?" Kay asked.

Lancelot recognised his presence again, turning a sombre face on him. "You would pay it?"

"Of course."

Briefly Lancelot betrayed a ghost of the contemptuous look he had worn when he spoke of Valerin. "You might think twice, Kay, when you learn what the ransom is. Valerin does not ask for gold or jewels. King Arthur's ransom is the sword Excalibur."

There was silence in the room. Briefly Gareth let himself think of what use Valerin could make of Excalibur. Did he mean to lead war against Arthur? Or to cut his way to Queen Guenevere through the defence of her knights? If his champion, the Golden Knight, could defeat Lancelot with an ordinary sword, Gareth's heart went cold to think what he might do with Excalibur.

"What will you do?" he asked Lancelot.

It was Kay who replied. "Lay siege to Valerin's castle." His voice had a satiric edge. "Or have all the Knights of the Round Table challenge this Golden Knight one by one, until Valerin gets tired of playing games, and slaughters King Arthur before our faces."

"And you have a better idea?" Lancelot asked.

"Kay, we can't give up Excalibur!" Gareth said, agonised.

Kay looked him up and down, fiercely disdainful. "You always did think with your guts, boy, not your head. Just as Lancelot does. Wait here." He went out through the far door, into the warren of stores behind the workroom.

Lancelot put a hand on Gareth's shoulder. "Pay no attention to Kay's insolence," he said. "He is so with everyone."

Gareth shrugged uncomfortably. He had not been offended; warmed, rather, by Kay snapping at him in the old way, reminding him of the days when he had been Kay's kitchen boy. It felt right, better than the chilly civility with which Kay had treated him ever since he returned from the first quest of his knighthood. And the warmth remained, with a flicker of hope, as he wondered what Kay had in mind.

When Kay returned he was carrying something long and slender, wrapped in sacking. He laid it on the table and folded back the wrappings. A sword lay there, fire waking deep in the stone in its hilt.

Gareth took a step forward. The sword looked like Excalibur. But Excalibur, he knew, must still lie in its place in the council chamber where the Round Table stood, where it always lay unless Arthur should take it up to ride to war.

"Years ago," Kay said, "Queen Morgan le Fay tricked her lover Accolon into fighting against King Arthur. She stole Excalibur and gave it to him, and left this in its place."

"Gawain told me the story," Gareth said. "I thought the false Excalibur was broken in the fight."

"It was." Kay grasped the hilt and drew the sword from its sheath; the blade flamed as it caught the firelight. "I had it reforged. I thought that one day a copy of Excalibur might come in useful."

Before he could sheathe the sword again, Lancelot reached out and took it from him. He stood, frowning, balancing the weapon, and swung it experimentally. "The weight is wrong," he said.

"Our foremost warrior would know that, of course," Kay said. "But since Valerin has never wielded the true Excalibur —"

"Wait," Lancelot said. "Are you suggesting that we offer this to Valerin? A false ransom for King Arthur?" His tone was grave, his expression disapproving.

Gareth saw a light spring into Kay's eyes, all his hawk's face focused on Lancelot. "You would prefer to hand him the true Excalibur? And then sit back to see what damage he could do with it?"

Lancelot stiffened. Gareth could see that the taunt had reached him, but he had himself under better control than Kay. "To offer the false for the true would be a lie," he said. "A knight who did so would lose his honour."

"And does your honour matter more to you than your king's life?" Kay asked scathingly.

Lancelot made no reply in words, but he handed the false Excalibur back to Kay and almost unconsciously brushed his hands together.

"Well, we can't ask the great Sir Lancelot to get his hands dirty," Kay said. "Don't worry, Lancelot. I'll go myself."

"You? Face Valerin?" Lancelot hardly bothered to hide his contempt.

Kay's lips twisted bitterly. "Since you would say I have no honour left to lose, who is better fit to do it?" More softly, almost to himself, he added, "I am… a tool just crude enough to be useful."

Gareth felt his heart torn. He glanced at Lancelot, who had drawn away, his disgust plain in his stance and the set of his head, though his face remained impassive. "Sir Kay," Gareth said, "I would beg a favour of you."

Kay faced him, his brows raised, his expression combative. "What favour?"

"Let me go with you. I'll ride as your squire, if you like."

He had the satisfaction of seeing Kay utterly astonished, bereft of words for the time it took Lancelot to speak.

"No, Gareth. You show your good heart, but any knight who joined with Kay in this would be tainted by his dishonour."

"You do not rule Sir Gareth," Kay said swiftly.

Gareth hid a smile. He had made his request without much hope, but Lancelot's opposition might be the one spur that would make Kay agree.

"No," Lancelot said. "But I may advise him. He is young, and lets his heart rule him. He will learn better. Or do you think it's my doing that no knights will ride with you, for fear of your evil tongue and ill repute?"

Kay made a convulsive movement with the sword.

"Don't," said Lancelot.

Kay stood rigid, then thrust the sword back into its sheath. He stood with head bowed, looking down at it.

"Kay?" Gareth said quietly. There was no response. "Kay, take me with you."

Kay turned to face him, the fierce look broken up into something Gareth could not read. His voice was acerbic. "And what would the honourable Sir Gareth say, if anyone asks him whether this is the true Excalibur?

"Me?" Gareth put on an expression of mock surprise. "Who would ask me? Who would expect a humble squire to know anything? And if they do," he added, "I shall just pretend to be stupid."

"You shouldn't find that at all difficult," Kay snapped.

He bundled the sword back into its wrappings and stalked out. Gareth grinned exultantly, tossed a few words of excuse in Lancelot's direction, and went to make ready.

Early next morning, Sir Kay and Gareth rode out of the city. Mist covered the valley; the horses seemed to wade in it. Kay's black Morial was restless, throwing his head from side to side, the jingle of his bridle the loudest sound in the still morning.

Kay himself was silent, shrouded in a black cloak. The false Excalibur, corded into its sacking covers, lay across his saddle.

"Sir Kay," Gareth began, knowing he was about to say the wrong thing, but preferring even that to saying nothing at all, "Are you sure you want to do this?" No reply. "When you come back, whether Arthur is with you or not, they'll say you lied and cheated —"

Kay reined in his horse and faced him. "If you don't want to associate with such a treacherous character," he said, "you had better go back. I'm sure you feel more at ease in Lancelot's company."

He jerked his head away, pain in every line of his face, and set Morial into motion again. Gareth followed. He dared not voice what he wanted to say: that he wanted to be where he was needed; that being at ease was not a knight's first duty. No words of his could assuage Kay's hurt and anger.

The sun was rising above the mists as the two horsemen passed beneath the outer trees of the forest. They followed the familiar path; Gareth was never sure when they passed from the everyday into the strange, from the known to the unknown. At first he thought that the sun had gone in, then that the forest was darker and thicker than he remembered. But soon he could see the change. He and Kay rode along a twisting alleyway; the walls were interlaced branches that joined overhead. To Gareth, the intertwining boughs and ivy tendrils and bindweed looked as complex as words written on parchment, but he did not know who might have the skill to read this living manuscript.

Little light fought its way through the mesh of branches, and their pace slowed. They were climbing, the path snaking back and forth across the face of the hill.

Mist curled through the gaps between the branches, but not like the white mist in the valley. This was black. It writhed across the path, a seething dark wall where half seen shapes formed and melted again into nothing. Gareth murmured a prayer, and made the sign of the cross. Riding a pace or two behind Kay, he could not read the older man's face, but he saw the stiff set of his shoulders and knew he was afraid.

The path suddenly levelled out, the barrier of trees left behind. A wind rose, blowing the mist into tatters. Ahead of them, the walls rough and shaggy with moss and fern as if they were a continuation of the crag, stood Valerin's fortress.

A gate was set into the wall, wrought from black steel. It stood open. On the pillars at either side were winged gryphons, looking as if they were carved out of black stone, but as Kay urged Morial towards the gate their wings arched, and they uttered a clanging cry.

Morial reared; Kay fought to control him. The horse stood still at last, quivering.

"Most castellans," Gareth said, "make do with a porter."

Kay gave him a fierce look and urged Morial on, skittering, reluctant, towards the gate. The gryphons cried out again as the knights passed through, but Gareth saw that they were tethered, with golden collars and thin golden chains.

At least, he thought, they're tethered now.

The gates led to a passage between walls of black rock, that after a few yards arched over and became a tunnel. It was smooth, sloping slightly downwards, and wide enough for Kay and Gareth to ride abreast. Lights in intricate golden housings hung from the roof.

Gareth was not sure how long they rode on. Kay kept silence, his gaze fixed on the path ahead, the glittering lights that curved gently into the distance. Glancing behind, Gareth saw the same curve, a necklace studded with light, the entrance lost in darkness. It was too easy, he found, to imagine that the curve might stretch on for ever, or loop back on itself, so that they would never find the way out.

At length they emerged into a vast chamber of stone, the roof supported by pillars soaring up like trees. Gareth was reminded of a great cathedral, even to the gathering of golden light at the far end, where the sanctuary lamp would burn perpetually over the altar.

The horses came to a halt as if at an unheard command. Gareth thought that a groom came to take hold of the bridle, but he could see no one. He exchanged a glance with Kay.

From the air, someone spoke. "My lord Valerin bids you dismount and approach his throne." The voice was soft, sibilant, with a timbre that suggested it did not need flesh or sinew or breath to form itself.

"Merciful God," Kay muttered.

He dismounted, clutching the false Excalibur. Gareth followed and stood at his side. The horses were led away. Briefly Kay stood still, a hand to his throat, and then strode forward towards the gathering of light.

Three shallow steps led up to a dais. On it was no altar but a golden throne, surrounded by stands where lamps were burning. The man who sat there was tall and slender, with the gold-brown skin Gareth had seen in holy icons. His hair was flat worms of gold. The stiff folds of his robe were encrusted with golden thread. He looked more like a statue than a living man.

Kay halted at the foot of the steps. "You are Lord Valerin?"

"I am Valerin, King of the Tangled Wood." The voice was a chime of golden bells. "Do you not kneel to me?"

"I kneel to no king but Arthur," Kay said brusquely.

Valerin leant forward. Now his voice was softer, mail-rings clashing together, liquid but still metallic. "You will kneel to me, if I wish it. Who are you, that come uninvited into my halls?"

"Uninvited?" Kay said. "Your... creatures –" He gestured into the darkness behind him – "seemed to expect our coming. I am Sir Kay, King Arthur's High Seneschal. I have brought his ransom."

He held out the false Excalibur. For a moment Gareth thought that Valerin looked startled, as if Kay had said or done something he had not expected. Then he raised one hand, in almost a ritual gesture. "Let me see."

Kay tugged at the cords and only managed to pull the knots tighter. He was not as self-possessed, Gareth knew, as he would like to appear. Gareth drew his belt knife and slashed the cords through, winning no thanks from Kay, who bundled the sacking into his hands and held out the sword, flat on his palms, to Valerin.

Valerin made no move to take it. "So that," he said, "is the great Excalibur."

"It is the price you asked," Kay said. He was crisp, unemotional, as if he was not aware that his honour died with the words, or knowing, he did not care.

Gareth's heart twisted in pity, though he clung to the right wooden expression for the unsuspecting boy he was pretending to be. There was something wrong with knightly honour, he thought, if it could not compass what Kay was doing now.

"Take the sword, Lord Valerin," Kay said. "And let me see king Arthur."

"Not yet," said Valerin. "You and I are not finished yet."

Fear clawed at Gareth. The road from the forest, this strange fortress, the disembodied servants and even Lord Valerin himself – all of that could be expected if men were forced to deal with sorcery. But this was something new.

"I have brought you your ransom," Kay said. "What more remains to do?"

"You have brought me Excalibur," said Valerin. "And now you must meet my champion. You will fight with him, and if you defeat him, then Arthur is free to go."

Gareth saw fury and fear together flare into Kay's face. He took a step forward. "That was not in the bargain."

"It is now."

"And what if I refuse?"

Valerin smiled, the first time any emotion had touched the graven face, a smile of cold amusement. "You have no choice, if you wish to see Arthur alive. Come, Sir Kay –" The voice pealed more strongly now – "surely even you can defeat my champion if you wield Excalibur?"

The unseen servants led Kay and Gareth to a small room off the great chamber. On a small table lay a suit of mail, with a white surcoat, a helmet and a plain white shield.

Gareth began helping Kay to arm. "Kay," he said hesitantly, "if you want, I'll do it." He braced himself, afraid that the suggestion would infuriate Kay.

The seneschal averted his face. "In God's name, Gareth," he said, "will you leave me without the last shred of honour? Do you think I'm a coward too?"

"No," Gareth said. "But this... thing, this Golden Knight – if it can defeat Lancelot..." His voice died away helplessly.

"Then it can defeat you," Kay said. "Besides, you're a squire here, you can't challenge a knight." His voice shook suddenly. "Thank God you can't."

He fastened on his sword belt with the false Excalibur, and put his own sword into Gareth's hands. "When it's over," he said, "if you can, take word to Lancelot and the queen. They must do as they think best."

"Kay –" Gareth began.

There was much he wanted to say, in friendship or farewell, but there was no time, and no encouragement from Kay to say even a part of it. He flashed one final look at Gareth, put on the helmet and went out: Sir Kay, lonely and indomitable, ready to face a knight, or a demon, who had already defeated Lancelot, with a sword that was not Excalibur.

Again the unseen servants guided them across the large central chamber to an opening at the far side. Their horses were waiting. They mounted, and rode down another passage that curved gently like the first, lit like the first with lamps of golden filigree.

After a few minutes a greenish gold light began to grow in front of them, and they rode out into what might have been a huge forest clearing, with sunlight filtering down through a canopy of leaves, if it had not been closed in with densely woven walls. Gareth sensed they were not in the open, but still somewhere in Valerin's fortress, under the weight of crushing pinnacles of stone.

At one side, on another raised throne, sat Valerin, poised and glowing golden as if he had just been poured from a craftsman's crucible. But Gareth's eyes immediately went to the other end of the clearing, where a mounted knight waited.

He wore golden armour. Light dazzled off the mesh of his mail shirt. His closed helmet was mirror bright, the plumes incandescent, red gold, almost aflame as if they were the feathers of the legendary phoenix. His shield was matt gold, without any device, and his surcoat just as plain. There was nothing to tell whether the golden knight was a living man, or some creature of sorcery.

A lance was driven into the ground not far from where Kay and Gareth had emerged. Gareth dismounted, fetched it, and gave it to Kay. Kay levelled it; the Golden Knight across the clearing did the same; Lord Valerin gave the signal, and the combat began.

Gareth could see one chance. Kay's outstanding skill was his horsemanship; in that alone Gareth thought him better even than Lancelot, and he had trained his Morial to obey the slightest touch. If Kay could unhorse the Golden Knight, so that the contest never came to a fight on foot, with swords, he might survive.

The horses rushed together. The knights clashed in the centre of the clearing. Kay's lance tip struck the Golden Knight's shield; the Knight rocked in the saddle, but kept his seat. Kay veered away; the Golden Knight's lance struck obliquely, raking across his shield. He rode on. Gareth remembered how to breathe.

The Golden Knight trotted his horse in a wide circle, controlling it ready for the next charge. The movement brought him close to Gareth. The golden helmet turned towards him, as if the eyes behind the slit contemplated him for a moment. Gareth could see nothing; he fought with the cold fancy that if he were to strip off the helmet and the golden armour, there would be emptiness beneath.

The horses' hooves pounded the turf as the riders came together a second time. Gareth watched Kay; he was balanced, controlled. His lance struck and shattered. Carried forward by the force of the thrust, Kay could not recover his seat. He slid to the ground; Gareth thought he would be trampled under the thundering hooves.

Morial galloped away towards the edge of the clearing. Kay, half stunned, was struggling to rise. The Golden Knight brought his horse to a standstill. He drove his lance point into the ground, dismounted and waited until Kay gained his feet. Kay drew the false Excalibur.

The swords clashed. Gareth made himself watch, in sick apprehension. On horseback there had been little to choose between the two knights. On foot the difference was obvious. Kay was matched with an opponent far beyond his skill, and the only question was how long his defeat would take.

Not long. The Golden Knight's sword flashed, and bright blood spurted from Kay's sword arm. Gareth cried out. For one horrible instant, he had thought the arm cut off.

Kay still held his sword, but as if he could barely raise the weight. He could not defend himself; he gave backward as the Golden Knight pressed hard on him, raining blows on his shield. Gareth thought the end had come.

Then Kay gathered himself, thrusting forward with his shield, using it to push his enemy off, and let go, so that the Golden Knight staggered under the impetus. In the brief respite, Kay changed his sword to his left hand.

The Golden Knight regained his footing, but he did not attack. Instead he dropped his shield, and changed his own sword from right to left as Kay had done.

Valerin started to his feet. Gareth's chest ached from the effort of breathing. He did not understand. Did the Golden Knight know honour, to fight an almost defeated enemy on fair terms? Was he not Valerin's creature, totally enslaved to his will?

The sword clashed again. Kay was clumsy now, moving slowly. The wound would weaken him, and he was not so skilful with the left hand. The Golden Knight should have been able to finish the combat within seconds. Instead, he parried Kay's strokes easily, but made no effort to break through his guard, as if this was a practice bout.

Then to Gareth's complete amazement, Kay sprang backwards, away from his adversary, and cast the false Excalibur aside. He pulled off his helmet, and cast that away too, and knelt defenceless before his enemy.

Gareth stared. It was not the ritual yielding on the defeated, still less a coward's last attempt to save his life. Rather it was a gesture of total submission, as if Kay did not care what would come after.

The Golden Knight grasped his sword in both hands. He raised it high above his head; the light caught it and turned it into a spear of molten gold. Then he brought it flashing down. But instead of a killing stroke, the sword rested lightly on Kay's shoulder, the touch of the accolade.

In that instant, everything changed. The interwoven walls of the clearing became flat, like tapestries in some great hall. Valerin himself, arrested in movement, was a figure stitched in gold thread. His shriek of rage was cut off, his face fixed in a silent howling.

Light shattered into a thousand splinters. The Golden Knight's armour began to dissolve. The ring mail melted to webs of gold and vanished. The helmet plumes whirled into nothing like sparks from a fire, and the helmet itself curled away like burning paper. As the glitter died from the air and Gareth's vision cleared, he found he was staring into the face of King Arthur.

He stood transfixed, until the cool movement of air against his face told him that Valerin's fortress had vanished utterly, and he stood once more in the forest. He ran across the clearing, and flung himself down at Kay's side.

Kay was lying in a faint, deathly white but breathing. Arthur stooped over him, cutting away the mail and shirt sleeve from the wounded arm. Without looking at Gareth, he said, "Have you anything to bind this?"

Gareth went back to his horse, which stood placidly cropping the grass, and brought salves, bandages and a waterskin from his pack. While he bound up the long, shallow gash down Kay's forearm, Arthur soaked a handkerchief and bathed Kay's face. His expression was intent, gentle. Gareth did not know what to say to him.

The bandage was in place before Kay revived. "He said quietly, "Arthur."

"Sir, how did you know?" Gareth asked.

Kay's eyes flickered towards him. "The king and I were boys together." He sounded exhausted, but quite lucid. "We fought together a thousand times. He made me practice like that, left-handed. How should I not know?"

Arthur raised his head and gave him a drink from the waterskin. "I was under enchantment," he said. "All I knew was to fight the men who came against me. One I defeated, then – I was standing over Kay, ready to give him his death blow. And I knew, suddenly, who and what I was."

"And the enchantment broke," Gareth said.

Kay sighed wearily and closed his eyes, resting against Arthur's shoulder.

"But what was it all for?" Arthur said. He listened in silence as Gareth told him all he knew. "Clever," the king said at last. "If Lancelot had killed me, Britain would have been without a king. If I had killed him, his kinsmen would have risen up in vengeance. The fellowship of the Round Table would have been destroyed. And with Excalibur, Valerin could have made himself king, with Guenevere as his queen. Very clever. I almost admire him. But he took no account of Kay."

He smiled affectionately down at Kay, who returned the look. Gareth had never seen him so tranquil. He found himself swallowing tears.

Then Arthur's smile faded to a frown. "Kay, the sword…"

Gareth got up and retrieved it from the forest floor where Kay had cast it away.

Arthur examined it. "Morgan's false Excalibur," he said. "Kay, you offered this for ransom? You lied to Valerin?" In the king's face a shadow grew of the same disapproval Lancelot had shown.

Kay's eyes widened; he sat up and moved away. His voice had grown defensive. "It was all I could see to do."

Arthur sighed. "Yes, Kay. I know it's hard. But we go on in honour, or there's little point in going on at all." He stood up and offered a hand to Kay. "Can you ride?"

"Yes." Kay ignored the hand, and struggled to his feet alone. He stood swaying; Gareth would have steadied him, but Kay wrenched violently away. "Go back to Lancelot." The words were spat out. "Tell him the story. Tell him that his precious honour would have brought Britain down in flames."

"Kay –" Gareth said, protesting.

Kay ignored him, and stumbled away across the clearing to where Arthur had mounted, and caught Morial's rein. Gareth did not try to make him listen; the only words that would do any good would have to come from Arthur, and he was silent.

The bond between the two men was strong enough to shatter Valerin's enchantment. But in common daylight neither of them could live with it. Arthur must be Arthur still, the noble king of an heroic band of knights. While Kay stubbornly refused to be a hero. Gareth's heart ached for him. He did not want Kay to be any different.

He was left with the false Excalibur in his hand. He was half inclined to pitch it into the nearest thicket, for it was quite useless. King Arthur's ransom had been, in the end, harder to pay: a man's honour, and his pain.

But Gareth could see that the sword might do harm in the wrong hands, so he fastened it to his own saddle. He mounted and brought up the rear, behind Arthur and then Kay, on the road back to Camelot.

The Flower of Souvenance

Sir Kay the Seneschal stood in the main courtyard at Camelot, inspecting the carts of merchandise that lumbered through the gates in the early morning. One of them was packed with bales of silk, a consignment badly needed for the next tournament.

"You're late," Kay said. "What excuse this time?"

The trader grinned, unimpressed by Kay's asperity. "This silk came from Cathay, sir. I don't need an excuse."

He cut the cords of one bale and pulled out a length of shimmering fabric for Kay to admire.

Just then, three armed knights, leading their horses, approached from the stable yard: Lancelot, Gawain, and Gawain's brother Agravaine.

"Kay," Gawain said, "we're going to ride a practice course at the tournament field. Do you want to come with us?"

"No," Kay said regretfully. "Too much to do."

"Then of your courtesy," Sir Lancelot said, "order this cart out of the gateway."

Suppressing irritation, Kay told the trader, "You know where to go. Ask for the Mistress of Embroidery. I'll come and speak to you later."

As the cart jolted off, Agravaine sniggered, "Sir Kay wields a needle better than a sword."

A haze of anger blurred Kay's vision. Without conscious thought, he drew his belt knife. He wanted nothing more than to plunge the blade into Agravaine's throat, to silence that sneering mouth.

He never knew if he would have done it; Lancelot was too quick. Darting in from the side, he seized Kay's wrist. Agony stabbed through Kay's arm; his fingers loosened, dropping the knife. Lancelot released him; the whole smooth movement had taken only seconds.

"You should think scorn, Sir Kay," Lancelot said, "to draw blade on your brother of the Table."

Kay's senses swam with pain. As his head cleared, he saw Lancelot holding out the dagger, hilt foremost. Behind him, King Arthur had appeared in the courtyard, and stood looking on.

"Merciful God, no…" Kay whispered.

Distressed, Gawain murmured an excuse, and drew his brother and Lancelot away. Arthur was left looking down at Kay, exasperation in his face. "Why is it, Kay, whenever there's a quarrel, I find you at the bottom of it?"

"Perhaps because you never look to the bottom of it!" Kay snapped, jamming the knife back into its sheath. "Once you would not –"

He broke off. He must never speak of that, the time when he and Arthur had been boys together, when they thought that they were brothers. He must never remind Arthur, for fear of what Arthur might think he meant to claim.

"Once you were not so… difficult." Arthur spoke more quietly, as if he understood what Kay had not dared say.

Kay felt tears welling up but he would not shed them. He tightened his mouth into a hard line.

"Once I was true knight," he said. "But no longer. They call me coward. My life has sunk to kitchen duties and accounts and inventories. There's no honour in it."

"Then what can I do?" Arthur's tone had grown more gentle.

Kay took a breath, hesitated, and said, "My lord, give me the next quest that is brought to court. Give me the chance to prove myself."

Arthur smiled, and gripped Kay's shoulder. "Willingly. You have my word."

Kay's heart became quieter, and he went about his duties more briskly with something to hope for, though with some misgivings when he wondered what the quest might be. He could not allow himself to fail.

The mid-day meal was almost over when a woman entered through the doors at the bottom of the hall. She stood in the space between the tables and made a deep reverence to Arthur.

"My lord," she said, "I come to ask your help."

She wore a gown and cloak of grey wool, neat and modest as befitted a serving-maid. She was no longer young, nor beautiful, but she spoke with quiet dignity. The hall grew silent.

"Speak," Arthur said. "No one in need is turned away."

The serving-maid approached the dais and held out a rose. Its petals were deep carmine, almost black at the heart. Around the stem a piece of parchment was rolled, fastened with gold thread.

"A flower of souvenance," Arthur said, smiling. "Does your lady invite us to some courtly diversion? Sir Gawain, this must be for you."

Gawain laughed, disclaiming. The serving-maid said, "This is no diversion, my lord, and the flower is more than it seems. Will you bid one of your knights to read my lady's letter?"

Arthur glanced back and forth along the table. Kay, whose misgivings had grown as he listened, said, "My lord, you promised me the next quest to come to court."

There was some laughter. Arthur looked taken aback, though still slightly amused. "True," he said. "If you wish for it."

The serving-maid went to Kay and gave him the rose. He laid it on the table while he unfastened the thread and unrolled the parchment. He read aloud, "My lord king, a strange knight has set up his pavilion outside my manor gates, and demands admittance.

He will allow no one to pass in or out. He says he will wed me, but I fear his thoughts lie another way. I pray you, send me a knight to overcome him, and I will reward him well. Lady Liane."

Kay let the parchment fall. There was some murmuring around the tables; he caught a ribald remark about what his reward might be. He thought the serving-maid had heard it too, for she said, still with the same dignity, "Your reward, sir, will be the rose itself. No knight who carries it can ever be defeated."

Now the murmuring held a note of wonder. Sir Lamorak's voice rose above it. "Kay, this quest must be yours. You need it more than the rest of us."

A bitter anger rose in Kay's heart. He caught up the rose. "I will accept it," he said. "It is my right. My lord Arthur promised it to me."

More comments, louder now, and laughter.

"You should test it," Agravaine sneered. "Even with the rose, Kay, would you dare fight Lancelot?"

"I'd even dare fight you, Agravaine," Kay said crisply. "Rose or no rose."

The clamour was rising. Arthur stilled it with a gesture. "Kay, is this what you want?" he asked. "What will you prove, if you win through sorcery?"

Kay knew that Arthur was right. But there was no going back. If he gave up the quest now, he would be branded a coward yet again. "This is the adventure God has sent me," he said, "and I will claim it."

Arthur sighed. "I do not like this." He raised a hand, cutting off Kay's protest. "Before I give you leave, I would see the power of the rose. Lancelot, would you fight a practice bout with Kay?"

Lancelot shrugged. "As you will, my lord. No honourable man would use enchantment in combat – but for practice, and to try the truth of this…"

He beckoned to a squire, and sent him to fetch two practice swords. Kay gave orders for the tables to be cleared away, and the rest of the knights drew back around the walls to leave a clear space for the two combatants. Arthur and Guenevere took their seats on the dais, and the serving-maid stood beside them.

Kay pinned the rose to his tunic. He hoped no one could see that his hands were shaking. Partly it was fear, the fear that any rational man would feel to be facing Lancelot, even in a practice bout, partly fury that Lancelot should speak so loftily about honour, as if his own life would bear scrutiny. He stood still, trying to present a stony face, trying to ignore the racing of his heart.

The squire returned with the weapons. Kay grasped the hilt and stepped forward to where Lancelot waited. That tall, loose-limbed figure and the bony, implacable face had sent better fighters than Kay fleeing in terror.

Kay was not sure what happened next. He saw everything more clearly. The two swords were edged with fire, as if the sun shone behind them. As Lancelot raised his weapon to counter Kay's stroke, Kay felt that time was stretching. He could see the one weak spot where he might strike, but instead he twisted his blade out of line, and sent Lancelot's sword flying out of his hand, skidding across the flagstones.

Kay had never seen before – and knew he would never see again – the utter disbelief on Lancelot's face. He strode across the hall and retrieved the sword, presenting the hilt to Lancelot across his arm. He said nothing; there was no need.

Around them the other knights were muttering in astonishment, mixed with hostility. Someone said, "Now try it without the rose."

Kay knew he was unpopular, knew that disarming Lancelot would not endear him to anyone. He did not care. It had been worth it, to see that look. "Mistress," he said to the serving-maid, "I claim the rose, and the right to free your lady from her oppressor."

"I thank you." She curtseyed to him. "But remember, sir, that with the rose comes the thorn."

King Arthur was looking anxious. "Kay," he said, "give this quest to Sir Lancelot, or Sir Gawain – someone who can overcome without enchantment. Otherwise, you ask for your own dishonour."

"Will you break your sworn word?" Kay flashed back at him.

Arthur's worried look deepened into a frown of displeasure. "That I will never do." His voice had hardened. "Take the rose, then, and the quest. But look for no honour when you return."

The sun was setting when Sir Kay came face to face with his adversary. The serving-maid, mounted on a white mule, had led him along unknown paths through the forest, and brought him as the afternoon waned to the edge of the trees.

In front of him, meadowland sloped gently down into a valley, where stood a moated manor house. The drawbridge was raised. Opposite the gateway was pitched a single pavilion, with a horse cropping the grass nearby.

The serving-maid pointed. "There is your opponent, sir."

Sir Kay glanced at her, raised one hand to touch the rose, fastened now to his helmet, and set spurs to his horse, black Morial. Before he reached the pavilion, the strange knight came out, armed save for his helmet.

"Who rides here without my leave?" he asked as Kay drew near.

"I am Sir Kay, High Seneschal of Britain. I need no man's leave to ride in Arthur's lands."

The knight threw back his head and guffawed. He was a huge man, taller even than Lancelot, and broader in the shoulders. He had a coarse-featured face, with wild yellow hair and beard.

"Sir Kay – yes, I've heard of you," he said. "What do you want? You can't be here to fight?"

Kay suppressed a furious retort. This was no time for combat with words; he needed to stay calm. The only answer he made was to strike with the tip of his lance the shield displayed outside the pavilion.

Still laughing, the knight put on his helmet and mounted. Kay trotted Morial away, expecting his adversary to do the same. The thundering of hooves warned him. He pulled Morial round to see the strange knight already galloping towards him, his lance in rest. Kay had barely time to level his own weapon before they clashed together.

Morial reared, hooves splaying out. That saved Kay, for the other knight's horse swerved, and his lance went wide. Kay's own lance caught the edge of his opponent's shield, but he rode on. Kay spurred Morial away, past the pavilion, until he had space to turn and ride the next course.

This time he was ready. He felt the same sharpening of the senses as when he faced Lancelot; everything was brighter, with harder edges, and he had all the time he needed to aim and strike.

At the last second, before the two knights met, Kay lay flat along Morial's neck. The strange knight's lance hissed over his head. His own lance struck true in the centre of the shield, flinging his opponent backwards from his horse. As Morial carried Kay onwards, he heard the crash as the knight hit the ground.

Sir Kay wheeled Morial and brought him to a halt. Swiftly he dismounted and drew his sword. His adversary was trying to rise, only to fall back and lie flat. As Kay approached, he held out a hand. "I yield, sir knight," he said. "I beg you, spare my life."

Kay stood beside the fallen knight and sheathed his sword. "Your life is safe from me," he said, "provided that you ride to Camelot and yield to the mercy of my lady Queen Guenevere. Tell her that Sir Kay sends you as her prisoner."

The courtly phrases slid easily from his tongue. Triumph spurted through his veins like liquid gold, as he imagined the stir of wonder when the knight announced himself before the court. But the triumph congealed to ice, because he knew that all the Knights of the Round Table, and Queen Guenevere and Arthur himself, would know that Sir Kay had won his victory only through enchantment.

He hauled the knight roughly to his feet. "Go quickly," he said.

The man stumbled off to where his horse was waiting, mounted, and rode away in the direction of Camelot. When he had disappeared into the forest, Kay took off his helmet and unfastened the rose. It still bloomed fresh and fragrant, as if it had been that moment plucked.

"You fought well, sir," a soft voice said.

Startled, Kay looked up. The grey clad serving-maid had silently ridden up beside him.

"No." Bitterness ate into his voice. "What would Sir Kay be without this? Here, take it."

The woman stepped back, refusing the rose. "No, sir. If you do not wish to keep it, you must return it to my lady yourself."

Kay looked at her, and then at the gates of the moated manor house. They stood open now, and someone had lowered the drawbridge. Fear stirred in him; the rose, he felt sure, would not protect him from what he might encounter there. He wanted nothing more than to let it fall and ride away.

"Very well," he said. "Take me to her."

The serving-maid led him across the drawbridge and through the gate into a courtyard. From there an arched passage led into a neglected garden where roses twined over crumbled masonry, but none so vivid as the rose he carried.

At one corner of the garden a door opened onto a passage and a spiral staircase. The serving-maid took Sir Kay as far as another door on the first floor, tapped and swung it open. "Lady Liane," she said.

Kay stood on the threshold. The room was small, a lady's solar, hung with tapestries. In a carved chair sat a lady, with her back to him, her head bent over a tapestry frame placed to catch the light from the window.

She was young, her slender body clothed in an embroidered gown, her hair a fall of golden silk. Kay could see her hands, expertly stitching, but nothing of her face. The serving-maid had vanished.

Kay's breath came faster. He raised a hand to his throat, swallowed, and said, "Lady, I am Sir Kay, King Arthur's High Seneschal. Your enemy is defeated, and you are free."

Lady Liane raised her head, but the flashing hands never paused. She said, "I thank you, Sir Kay."

Her voice was low and musical. Kay hesitated. He did not know how to continue. He was clumsy enough when he could talk with court ladies face to face; this encounter defeated him entirely. He began, "Lady, the rose..."

"Is yours, sir, if you wish it."

"I do not, lady, though I thank you."

He took a pace into the room and held out the rose. Lady Liane did not turn to take it.

"Not?" The voice was amused now. "Do you not wish to smite your enemies, sir, and you a knight? Or vanquish all contenders at the tournament, and win the crown for your lady?"

"I have no lady," Kay said harshly, and then, with daring he could not account for, "Let me see your face."

The hands stopped their swift, precise movements. For a second Lady Liane was utterly still; then she rose and turned towards him. Sir Kay gasped and recoiled, barely restraining himself from making the sign of the cross.

Lady Liane held her head proudly. Her face was eaten away, by plague or some vile enchantment; yellowing sinews were stretched over bone, the mouth a crude gash, the nose a beak of some predatory bird. It was the face of something long dead, except for the eyes, still living, clear and grey and lovely.

"Well, sir?"

The exquisite voice from the horror of a face drained the last of Kay's courage. He found no words to reply. There was no reply, save weeping. He stood frozen, still holding out the rose.

As if he had questioned her, Lady Liane said, "I was one of Lady Nimue's maidens. I desired too much of her magic. I wished to be so beautiful that the best knights in the world would contend for my favours." The lipless mouth twisted. "A foolish dream. Lady Nimue could not undo what I had done, but she gave me the rose."

She drew closer to Kay; he managed not to flinch. Her hand hovered over the petals, but did not touch. "It is a flower of souvenance, sir. A courtly trifle, a lady's game. But it is, truly, a flower of memory. It restores the past. Was there no time, once, when Sir Kay's reputation stood higher than it does now?"

If Kay had closed his eyes, he might have believed she smiled. He cleared his throat, forcing out his answer. "Once... by Humberside, in the Queen's defence, I killed two kings with one lance. But those days are long gone."

"Not if you keep the rose, sir. It will not fade or wither. It is yours if you claim it."

Kay could not deny temptation. The rose filled his vision – those velvet petals, the living carmine with the death's head as their background. His senses were swirling away in its heady perfume.

He could return to Camelot with the rose. He could defeat them all, even Lancelot. He would be the first knight of the Table, the Queen's champion, at Arthur's side as he had once been...

But he could hear the mockery still. His victories would win no honour, because everyone would know that they came from enchantment. The rose would drive him even further from Arthur, because with it he would become something that Arthur could not acknowledge. He heard again the voice of the serving-maid: "Remember, sir, that with the rose comes the thorn."

"No, lady," he managed to say. "I wish for no reward. Take your own again."

Lady Liane sighed, and took the stem from his hand. As a crystal glass is filled with wine and takes colour from it, beauty flowed into her face. Soft skin covered bone and tendon, lips grew red as the petals, thick lashes fringed her eyes. She stood before him young, lovely, quivering with life.

"Merciful God!" Kay whispered. "And you would have given this to me? When you could stand, as you are now, beside any lady in the land, and be courted for your beauty?"

Lady Liane smiled now, but there was a hint of bitterness in it. "Sir Kay grows a sweet tongue. But what is beauty to me? Is it any more real than your skill? Or just a memory of what once was? Would any knight say he loved me if he saw me as I really am?"

She tucked the flower into the bosom of her gown, and turned back to her tapestry. "Farewell, sir," she said.

"Can I do no more to serve you?"

"Only by leaving. And by saying nothing of this when you return to Camelot."

Sir Kay bowed to her, though she did not see him. He tried to find something more to say, but achieved only a shaken farewell. He went out, passing the serving-maid at the foot of the stairs, through the tangled garden and the courtyard. Outside, Morial waited. A chill wind had come with the twilight; Kay was shivering as he mounted.

There would be duties at Camelot, even after so short an absence. He could cope with the sneering comments that would undoubtedly greet him. Though he was no fighter, there was consolation in being, as he knew, a superbly efficient seneschal.

But as he rode away, he could not help turning to look once more at the manor gates, closed again by some unseen hand. What consolation there? On all the road back to Camelot, Sir Kay could find no answer to that question.

The Trial of Sir Kay

That year, Arthur held his All Hallows' Court at Carlisle. Sir Gawain of Orkney, as he waited in the great hall for the serving of the midday meal, was well aware of the king's reasons, and not convinced in his own mind that they were good ones.

The Northern Kings had never paid homage willingly, had never been friendly to Arthur, who had come among them with goodwill, hoping to know them better and to gain their confidence. Gawain, seeing the way in which the members of the various retinues were eyeing each other, thought the Court was more likely to end in murder.

Meanwhile, he was waiting restlessly upon Arthur's custom of hearing of a marvel or an adventure before he would begin the meal.

"Kay," he said to his neighbour at the table, "when you're in charge at Camelot, how do you manage to have everything running so smoothly, with all this waiting about?"

"Practice," Sir Kay replied laconically.

Sir Gareth, Gawain's brother, leant eagerly across the table. "Tell me," he said. "Do you ever... well, go out looking?"

Kay's mouth twitched. "You aren't supposed to ask that."

Gareth laughed delightedly, and the sound attracted the attention of the group of men next to them, strangers, who all wore the livery of the same lord.

"Arthur's men?" one of them asked.

He was a young man, with greasy red curls, his thick-set body already running to fat; for all that, he looked and sounded dangerous.

Gawain bowed his head with infinite courtesy. "Yes," he said. "Sir Gawain of Orkney, at your service, gentlemen. My brother, Sir Gareth. Sir Kay, King Arthur's seneschal."

The young man's eyes narrowed as he looked at Kay. "Sir Kay," he said. "We've heard of you, Sir Kay. Your fame has spread even this far."

Gawain felt Kay stiffen, but he said nothing, and sat with his eyes fixed on the tablecloth.

The young man leant forward. "We've heard that you're one of the first knights of Arthur's court – when it comes to running away."

Kay reached to where his sword would have been.

Gawain's hand clamped hard around his wrist. "Don't!" he whispered urgently. "They're looking for a quarrel. If we strike the first blow, Arthur will be blamed for it."

Kay nodded almost imperceptibly. He had gone white, and his lips were compressed. Across the table, Gareth, warned by the shake of his brother's head, bit back an angry protest.

The red-haired young man smiled. "You might be some use back in Camelot," he said. "For scraping bowls or counting loaves of bread. But up here – no use at all. I wonder Arthur goes to the trouble of bringing you."

Gawain's grip on Kay's wrist must have been painful, but when he saw Kay's eyes, hot and desperate, he wondered how much longer he could go on keeping him silent. Kay had already endured more insult than any man should be asked to bear; for the fiery Kay, the effort at self-control was truly heroic.

To Gawain's great relief, before anyone else could speak, there was a stir at the door of the hall and a voice shouting for silence. In the arched opening appeared a lady, veiled in a dark cloak and riding a white mule. As the noise in the hall died down, she dismounted, entered, and advanced into the clear space between the tables. She raised slender hands to put back the hood of her cloak; Gawain saw how beautiful she was.

"My lord king!" Her voice was clear and confident. "I beg you, grant my request."

Arthur signed for her to continue.

Good, Gawain thought. Perhaps now he'll fulfil his custom and we can all eat. Give that lout something to think about beside baiting Kay.

At his side he felt Kay begin to relax, and released the grip on his wrist.

The lady was explaining how a strange knight had challenged her father, who was too ill to meet him. "I ask for a champion from your court, my lord," she said. "Everyone knows that the knights of King Arthur are the finest in the world."

There was some murmuring at that, but the king looked pleased. "Of course," he said, and glanced around the tables. "Who will go with the lady?" he asked. "Lancelot? Gawain, perhaps…"

Instantly Kay was on his feet. "My lord, please let me go."

As Arthur looked at him, there was a flicker of surprise in his face, immediately suppressed; Gawain knew that Kay would not have missed it.

Urgently he repeated, "Please, my lord!"

The king hesitated for a moment longer, and then nodded. "Very well, Kay. Thank you. You had better make ready to go."

Kay withdrew from the table without a word to his friends, or a glance towards the man who had insulted him. Gawain saw him pause for a few words with the lady, and then leave the hall; she sank in a low curtsey to the king, and followed.

Gawain watched her go, frowning a little. He felt uneasy; he felt even more uneasy when he saw the gloating look on the face of the red-haired man. Was it just coincidence, Gawain asked himself, that he had ridiculed Kay, accused him of cowardice and incompetence, and even questioned his right to a place at Arthur's table, just before the opportunity had come for Kay to prove to everyone that he was wrong?

While the servants were bringing in the first course of the meal and everyone had begun to forget the incident, Gawain leant across the table to Gareth. "I don't like this," he said.

"You don't think Kay is a coward, do you?" Gareth asked indignantly.

Gawaine smiled; Gareth had a strong protective streak towards Kay. "No, of course not," he said. "But this – it's too pat, too easy. Almost as if it was arranged. I don't think Kay is going to find what he expects to find. Gareth," he went on softly, "suppose we follow them? At a discreet distance?"

"A very discreet distance," Gareth agreed. "If Kay finds out, he'll kill us!"

They withdrew quietly from the hall, collected their swords and had their horses saddled. It was still early on a cold, misty afternoon. They followed the white road that wound down the hill, away from the fortress, in the direction the gate guard told them had been taken by Kay and the lady.

The road crossed a stretch of moorland and then plunged into a tract of forest. Nothing moved along it; the world was utterly empty. Gawain let his horse move at an easy trot. Kay would be held up by the pace of the lady's mule, and Gawain had no wish to catch him, at least not before he had a better idea of what was happening.

Not until they were approaching the forest was there movement on the road. A horse broke out from the trees, riderless, wild, its reins broken.

"Kay's horse!" Gareth exclaimed.

The horse went careering off across the moorland, and they did not try to catch it. Gawain pressed forward now, with Gareth close behind him, his uneasiness sharpened to a desperate anxiety.

It was darker beneath the trees, quieter, the horses' hooves muffled by fallen leaves. Gawain called Kay's name, but there was no reply. They moved more slowly, scanning the trees on either side in case they should miss some clue to what had happened, but when it came, it would have been impossible to miss.

The undergrowth had been broken down, trampled over a wide circle that included the road. There was a sharp tang of bruised grasses in the air.

Gawain dismounted. "Kay!" he called again.

There was still no reply. He began to search, back and forth across the circle, while Gareth walked his horse on as far as the next bend in the road. Gawain began to dread what he might find.

Kay was lying at the edge of the circle, under a tree. In the failing light, his dark tunic blended into the shadows. He lay prone, sprawled with his face to the ground. Kneeling beside him, Gawain could make out an ugly, ragged gash in his side, a spear head and a few inches of splintered shaft still jutting from the wound. The dead leaves where he lay were clotted with blood.

Shaking, Gawain turned him over. His face was pale, streaked with blood. His eyes were closed. At first Gawain thought he was dead, but blood still oozed from the wound, and when Gawain drew his belt knife and held the bright blade close to Kay's lips, it was stained by the faint exhalation of his breath.

Gawain straightened up. "Gareth!" he called. "Come here!"

Sir Kay lay half sunk among the pillows, his face white as the linen, beneath tumbled dark hair. The short winter day had drawn to an end; a single lamp burned beside the bed.

Watching, Gawain saw Kay's eyes flutter open, dark and unfocussed. Gently he raised his friend's head and held a cup of water to his lips.

Kay drank; gradually his eyes lost that terrifying vacancy. "Gawain?" he whispered.

"Yes, I'm here."

"Then why…" The wisp of sound died away.

Gawain set the cup aside and let Kay lie back again. Kay was frowning in a vague perplexity.

"There was a knight…" He began to turn his head restlessly from side to side. "We fought, and he –" He caught his breath. "Gawain, the lady! Where is she?"

Impossible to lie to him. Gawaine shook his head. "I don't know. You were alone when we found you. They're out looking –"

"Oh, merciful God!" The words were sobbed out. "I pledged my word… Gawain, I must get up."

He attempted to rise, pushing aside the blankets and furs, but the effort proved too much, leaving him limp and gasping.

Gawain eased him back onto his pillows, where he lay trembling. "You're hurt; lie still," Gawain said.

Kay's eyes sought for his, still keenly intelligent; even the pain of his wound could not dull the knowledge of how disastrously he had failed. "You need not stay," he said, and turned his head away.

For answer, Gawain reached out and took his hand. For a moment, feebly, Kay tried to free himself from the patient clasp, and then gave in.

Gawain went on sitting there, in silence, listening to the buffeting of the wind outside. Kay was drifting from consciousness again, his eyes half closed, Then footsteps sounded outside; the door was flung back, and Kay roused again at the noise.

"Dear God, Gareth!" Gawain said irritably. "Can't you do anything quietly?"

His brother closed the door carefully behind him. He was panting as if he had run up the stairs. He brought a gust of the cold outdoors with him; fine rain misted on his hair and the fur on his cloak. There was a wild look about him that quickened all Gawain's apprehensions.

"What is it?" he asked.

"Is there news?" Kay's weakness made his urgency all the more painful. "The lady – is she found?"

"Yes, found," Gareth replied. "At home, in her father's manor."

Kay let out a shuddering sigh, and Gawain murmured a prayer of thankfulness, while still wondering why Gareth should look so distraught. "Tell us," he said.

"It was getting dark," Gareth began, "and I'd given up the search. I started to make my way back, and when I got to the road, I came up with a knight riding this way, and I asked him if he'd seen her." He had been speaking swiftly; now his voice faltered a little. "He said he was her father."

"Miraculously recovered from his illness," Gawain interposed.

Gareth knelt down beside Kay, and put a hand on his shoulder. "Kay, listen… I don't believe this, and I don't think anyone else will believe it either. But he said – he said he rode out to meet her, and found her in the forest with a knight – Kay, I'm sorry – a knight who had raped her, and he fought with him, and then took his daughter home and was coming to the king to ask for justice. I told him –"

Again Gareth broke off, as Kay, who had listened to him with a fierce, unwavering attention, suddenly gave way, all strength leached out of him, his eyes closing, his head slipping to one side.

"Dear God, I've killed him!" Gareth exclaimed, beginning to chafe Kay's hands frantically.

Gawain turned aside to pour a little wine into a cup. "You're a fool, Gareth," he said. "You didn't need to tell him, not yet, at least, not until –"

"No." It was Kay who interrupted, very weak, but struggling back to consciousness. "No, I want to know, or how can I –" He pressed a hand to his lips. "What am I going to do?"

Gawain heard only a cry of desperation, but Gareth chose to answer the question. "The usual thing would be to challenge him," he said. "Let him prove what he accuses you of, if he dares. But as it is –"

"Kay can't fight him like this."

"I can if I have to." His mouth was set; Kay at his most obstinate.

Gawain almost smiled. "Dear Kay, I don't think you could walk as far as that door, much less fight. But it doesn't matter. You don't have to. Appoint a champion in your place. I'll do it for you. I'll be glad to."

Kay was staring at him. "Oh, no," he said. "I won't involve you in my trouble, Gawain."

Gareth, who by now was sitting on the side of the bed, smiled down at him, and gathered Kay's hands into his own. "Let me do it, then. There's nothing to worry about. Gawain or I could get the better of him in five minutes. Or you could ask Lancelot," he went on, growing enthusiastic. "Lancelot wouldn't even need five minutes. One look from Lancelot… Oh, Kay, dear Sir Kay, don't!"

His voice changed to distress as Kay turned his head aside, tears spilling over uncontrollably. "I was never kind to you," Kay gasped out. "And you haven't asked me, either of you…"

For a moment they were both bent over him, comforting, reassuring, trying to call him back from the dark places he had chosen.

Gawain could not help realising that there were plenty of people in the court who would believe, or pretend to believe, the charge against Sir Kay. But for himself, it was absurd to imagine that Kay would rape the lady he had given his word to serve. Kay's integrity might not be the conventional chivalry of Arthur's court, but it was very real and deep-rooted.

At last Kay won his battle for self-control, though the effort was beginning to exhaust him. "I won't let you fight for me," he said, the old irascibility creeping back into his voice. "Even if you defeat this man, even if you kill him, you won't kill the lie. People will still think I did this – this foul…" Disgust choked off the words.

"The king will never believe it," Gareth said.

Kay's hands clenched. Gawain knew that Gareth, without realising it, had pierced to the heart of Kay's fears.

"If he does believe it," Kay said, with such desolation that Gawain thought his heart would break, "then I don't care what happens to me."

Once Kay had gone to sleep, Gawain brought a fur rug and a blanket, and settled himself beside his bed. In the middle of the night he was roused by Kay crying out.

"Arthur – oh, Arthur, no!"

He was tossing in an evil dream, his face flushed, his body at fever heat. When Gawain gave him a drink he half woke and muttered something incoherent. Gawain brought a bowl of water and bathed his forehead until he sank into a quieter sleep. In the early morning, when Gareth came to relieve him, Gawain went to see the king.

Arthur kept him waiting. The ante-room was crowded with the followers of the northern kings, and when Gawain entered there was some whispering, and sidelong, hostile glances. Gawain ignored it all, and went to sit in the window seat, uncomfortably feeling their eyes boring into his back.

At length he was called into the king's private room, and saw to his infinite relief that Arthur had dismissed his servants, so that they could talk alone. Arthur was pacing, the tawny lion, deceptively weary and slow-moving, but he motioned Gawain to a seat.

"My Lord, I want to talk about Kay."

Arthur nodded; he must have realised that. "You've been with him, haven't you?" he asked. "I'm glad of that." He sounded as if he was having difficulty admitting it. "I'm glad he isn't alone."

"It's you he wants, my lord."

The great head swung round towards him; Gawain could almost see sparks flying off the red-gold hair. The amber eyes shone.

"Gawain, one of my men is accused of a foul crime, and if I don't see that justice is done, we'll have the whole of Britain in flames. You saw them out there? Just waiting for an excuse."

He paced again.

Gawain eyed him, and tentatively asked the one question that he had to ask. "My lord – you surely don't believe it?"

Arthur stood still, his back to Gawain. Gawain found that he was terrified of seeing his face when he turned. But the king remained motionless, and the answer when it came was unexpectedly mild.

"I've known Kay all my life. I know exactly what he's capable of. And rape isn't on the list. But he stands accused. I can't ignore that. I can't prove that this man – the girl's father – is lying, and of course I couldn't be so uncivilised as to expect to speak to the girl herself!" He gave a short, humourless laugh. "You know, Gawain, I think it was planned – everything that happened yesterday – to trap Kay."

He moved over to the window and stood looking out. Gawaine felt the pressure of his power, hemmed in and restricted, and knew that it would break out but for the conscious effort of his will.

"He was used," Arthur went on. He smiled sadly. "It's easy enough, God knows, to work out how Kay will react. And he's so perfect for their purpose! He's High Seneschal, but that goes with my favour. Of himself, he's not particularly wealthy or powerful. And not a dangerous man; they might have thought twice before they played their games with Lancelot, or even with you. But Kay was brought up as my brother. The one man I might be expected to protect. And if I do so – then what has it meant, all this talk of law and justice in my kingdom? Worth less than the dust on the wind! They will rebel, Gawain, if I make the slightest mistake."

He stood with his hands against the window embrasure. Gawain waited, expecting to be dismissed, but when Arthur turned back to him, it was to ask, "How badly hurt is Kay?"

"The wound itself wouldn't kill him, my lord." Gawain was choosing his words carefully. "But he needs rest, and instead he's fretting himself into a fever." He hesitated, and then went on, "He's afraid you will believe him guilty."

Arthur slammed his fist against the wall, and stood rigid, his eyes closed. Gawain, shaken by the swift uncoiling of passion, would not have been surprised to see the wall start to crumble.

Very quietly, Arthur said, "I am the king. I may not –"

"It isn't the king he wants."

If Gawain had thought about it, he would never have dared to interrupt. But the words were out, and Arthur was looking at him with a sudden daunting intensity.

The king drew a deep breath, and relaxed. "Very well," he said. "Come."

He scoured through the ante-room like the wind off an icefield; following, Gawain heard the babble of speculation breaking out behind him. Too late to worry about what he had set in motion; was it, after all, the first stirrings of war?

In Kay's room, he and Gareth were talking quietly; they broke off as Arthur entered. Gawain saw Kay's eyes dilate. His voice quivered with a desperate urgency. "My lord, oh, my lord, you shouldn't be here!"

Standing by the door, Gawain could not see Arthur's face, but he could hear the warmth, strong and vibrant, as he said, "Brother, you're talking nonsense. Now tell me what really happened, and then we can decide what we're going to do."

Not knowing whether he wanted to smile or weep, Gawain beckoned Gareth out of the room, and closed the door softly behind them.

When Gawain returned, the king had gone. Kay lay still; he looked up as Gawain came in, and smiled peacefully.

"Is everything all right?" Gawain asked.

"Oh, yes," Kay murmured.

His tranquillity was a complex, precarious balance between opposing demands. Gawain wanted to ask what the king had said, but he was reluctant to intrude on Kay's privacy. He was beginning to speak when Kay interrupted him.

"I have agreed to a trial by ordeal."

"What?" Gawain strode round the bed, bent over Kay and seized his hands urgently. "Kay, that's barbaric! Surely Arthur didn't ask you –"

"No, I suggested it." Kay sighed faintly. "Gawain, you know that if Arthur ignores the law to protect me, he will lose his hold on the kingdom. How can I ask him to go to war for my sake? This castle is seething with men who were his enemies, and will be again, given the slightest excuse."

"And one of them planned this," Gawain said.

Kay gave him a twisted smile. "And I fell in with his plans. Oh, I know how I let them use me. I'm not proud of myself, Gawain. So it's only right that I should do this."

Gawain sat back and looked at him. He thought of Kay – practical, logical Kay – submitting himself to the crude torment of a trial by ordeal. His mind shied away from the picture. And yet God should protect the innocent. Did that mean, Gawain wondered, that his faith was not strong enough, or simply that he refused to believe in a God who could connive in such savagery?

He asked the question that was sticking in his throat. "What must you do?"

"I don't know. Arthur will consult with the other kings, and the bishop. It doesn't matter. I'm not afraid." He had a strange, distant look, as if he was drifting too far away for Gawain to reach him. "You know, Gawain," he went on, almost dreamily, "I don't think this wound is going to heal. If I fail the ordeal, there isn't a great deal more that Arthur can do to me." He closed his eyes and then opened them again. "No, there is one thing that frightens me. I'm afraid that my strength will give way, so that I can't do what they ask of me."

Gawain felt as if an aching wound had opened in his throat. Quietly, he asked, "Do you want me to help you?"

The question pierced Kay's hard-won serenity, threatening to shatter it. "You would…?" He was staring, his eyes brilliant, knowing what a bitter thing Gawain was offering for the sake of friendship. "No," he whispered. "I won't have you tainted along with me."

Gawain bent and kissed his forehead. "You're not," he said. "And I'll be there. Go to sleep."

By the time the summons came from the king, Kay had rested, and found from somewhere the strength to get out of bed and dress. The rules of the ordeal asked for him to be barefoot, bare-headed, and wearing a white, penitential garment. Kay had chosen a robe of stiff, figured silk, belted and fastened with pearl and silver; he looked magnificent, and about as penitent as a wild hawk.

It was a sombre day, cloudy and raw with cold. The king and his court, the visiting kings and their retinues, the bishop and his acolytes, had assembled outside the castle. They looked like a great, restless flower border, blazing against the grey walls. The shifting mass of colour, the murmuring of many voices, all grew still, as Kay approached.

Gawain slipped into his place near the king, beside Gareth. Not far away, at the foot of a gentle slope, a long strip had been cut out of the turf to make a shallow pit of burning charcoal; a sullen pall of smoke hovered a few inches above it.

"They want him to walk across that," Gareth said, revulsion vibrating in his voice. "Gawain, can't you stop it?"

Gawain dared not look at him. "If we try," he said, "we'll have a war on our hands."

The bishop was waiting at the king's right hand, and on his left was a tall, grey-haired man whom Gawain had not seen before.

"The lady's father," Gareth told him.

Sir Kay stood before them, his head held high. He should have knelt; Gawain knew perfectly well that if he had tried he would probably not have got up again, but the impression he gave was of overwhelming arrogance.

Arthur had a strange, shuttered look, as if his spirit was somewhere else. He said something in a low voice to Kay, and then the bishop spoke, as if he was instructing Kay what to do; Gawain caught only the last few words.

"…and we trust that God will defend the right."

"You are to be congratulated, my lord," Kay said, "on the strength of your faith." He paused for a moment, eyes snapping out a challenge, and then went on, his voice raised so that everyone could hear it. "I swear before you, my lord king, and before Christ, that I am innocent of this charge against me."

Turning, not hesitating, he began to walk towards the pit. Gawain watched with a sick apprehension, nothing coherent in his mind any longer. Beside him, he heard Gareth murmuring a prayer. Then a few paces from the pit Kay's firm step faltered; he pressed a hand to his side and Gawain saw a scarlet blotch beginning to spread against the silvery white of his robe. The wound had broken open. Kay hesitated, took another two or three steps, stumbling now, and then crumpled to the ground a pace or two away from the edge of the pit.

There was a stir among the crowd. Somebody close to Gawain said, "Oh, beautifully done!" Remembering his promise, Gawain started forward, not knowing what he meant to do, but, before he reached Kay, his friend struggled onto hands and knees, dragged himself the last few feet, and collapsed on his face among the smouldering coals. Flame sprang up around him.

"Dear God!" Gawain sobbed out.

Unthinking, he flung himself into the pit, grabbed at Kay's shoulders and began to lift him, before his senses broke through his desperation and he began to understand.

He knelt on the coals, with Kay in his arms. There was no heat. Around them, flames rose in a golden wall, a shimmering calyx of fire. Kay's face and hands were unhurt; there was not even a mark on the white robe. Beginning to revive now, he was blinking in confusion, shrinking against Gawain even as fear gave way to awe. In silence, in light, the world was changed.

Gawain was never sure how long they crouched there, clinging together. Outside, it might have been no more than a few seconds; within the fire, time had burnt away, and there was only eternity. Kay, leaning back against Gawain's shoulder, stirred, and sat up, a hand at his side where the spear had driven home. The scarlet stain on his robe had disappeared.

"Kay..." Gawain could not go on.

"It is... healed."

His eyes met Gawain's, his gaze lost in wonder. Around them, the sheet of flame began to sink, to break up, as the world pressed in again.

Kay's expression changed. "Gawain!" His voice was low, fierce. "What do you think you're doing here? You must be out of your mind, you could have killed yourself –"

Laughing, Gawain rose to his feet and pulled Kay with him. "Kay!" he broke in. "Spitting like a wildcat! Now I know you're well again."

He urged Kay back onto the turf as he felt heat begin to rise from the pit. Outside the castle walls, flakes of colour began to break away from the mass of courtiers, as people hurried down to meet them.

Gareth was the first. "The king wants to see you," he announced, flinging an arm across Kay's shoulders.

Kay drew a long breath, his hand at his throat, and glanced back at the pit. "I'd rather walk across there again," he said. Hurriedly, half ashamed, he added, "For God's sake, stay with me."

"You don't need to ask," Gawain said, with a pang of pure joy that he had asked. God was very good, he thought, and there was more than one kind of miracle.

Together, in the few seconds before the crowd engulfed them, they began to walk up the slope to meet the king.

Sir Kay's Grail

Sir Gawain of Orkney stepped out through a narrow door onto one of the topmost battlements of Camelot and saw, a pace or two away, the man he was looking for.

Sir Kay stood with his hands flat on the parapet, looking out, and down. His stance almost suggested that he meant to lever himself upwards and spring into the void.

Gawain shivered. He took the step that brought him to Kay's side, and said lightly, "Whatever are you doing up here?"

Kay's head jerked towards him; he was surprised into an unexpected smile. He had not changed at all in the months Gawain had been away – the head erect, the face keen, almost challenging – unless perhaps silver sifted more thickly in his black hair.

"I didn't know you were back," he said. "When did you get here?"

"Oh, about an hour ago." Gawain clasped the hand Kay offered him. "I'd have found you before, if you hadn't been crawling around up here, like a pigeon."

"Pigeons don't crawl," Kay said pedantically. "I've been looking at the condition of the stonework," he explained, rubbing powdery mortar between thumb and forefinger. "I need to send some masons up here. Otherwise one night soon we'll find the castle crumbling around our ears."

He laid his hands on the parapet again, and Gawain stood beside him. A quick glance down showed the castle falling away beneath him like a precipice, to where the river creamed far below. Beyond the river were the tumbled roofs of the city, houses huddled together within the retaining wall, and beyond that a swell of hillside, the dark line of the forest, and a loop of the road Gawain had travelled not long before.

Gawain wondered if Kay often stood here, watching the road with its comings and goings, hungering for the challenge that comes with freedom.

"Is all well?" he asked.

Kay sighed, and leant against the parapet, grey stone mottled with acid yellow lichen. "No. But it's no worse." He made a quick, impatient movement, his falcon's face sharp with pain. "We're too peaceful," he said. "The young men, some of them, they've never known anything else. God forbid that I should wish for war. I've seen men die – too many of them. But now – it's all gossip and sniggering behind doors, and rumours scurrying about like lice –" He broke off with a disgusted sound in his throat.

Gawain was smiling sadly. "Poor Kay," he said. "The rest of us come and go; you're tied here."

Kay looked at him, brows raised, disdain to his fingertips. "By duty; yes, I'm Seneschal. Don't pity me. The job preserves my sanity. I think I'd be afraid to leave, and not know what I would find when I came back. But I'm tired, Gawain, deathly tired."

He turned away, resting his arm along the parapet, and stared out across the city. Gawain understood what he had left unspoken, caught through his eyes that trinity of Arthur, Lancelot, and the Queen, sensed the perilous balance that could so easily be destroyed.

As if Kay was following his thoughts, he said, "You would be surprised how much good you can do by changing the conversation." A hint of amusement crept into his voice. "Especially if you aren't overburdened with a reputation for courtesy. Or I can send for the latest harper, or suggest a game of chess. An excellent game, chess."

"You're an excellent player."

Kay turned back to him. A smile was curling the corners of his mouth. "My king has been in check more times than I care to count," he said. "But not checkmate, please God, not yet."

He took Gawain's arm, and they walked slowly along the battlements.

"Tell me your news, Gawain," Kay asked.

"Little enough. They say the Grail has been seen again."

"They've been saying that for twenty years."

"Yes, but this time…" Gawain frowned, remembering. "I rode through Astolat. There was a girl there, a weaver's daughter. She saw the Grail, and fell down in a fit, and prophesied. I spoke to her myself."

"And was it true?" Kay asked. His sceptical, sardonic look was back.

"I don't know. She believed it. More than that, I can't say."

"The Grail, if it exists," Kay began, "belongs in Sarras, in the Holy City, and no one can tell us what road would lead us there." His voice had held an edge of sarcasm, that faded as he went on, in a kind of wistful longing. "Suppose we looked down from these battlements, Gawain, and found ourselves there? What would we see? Gates of pearl, walls of amethyst? And the light… And healing." He covered his face with his hands. His voice was stifled. "But there's darkness all around us. And our wounds go on festering. If the Grail did show itself, why should it come here?"

Appalled by the sudden revelation of the misery and disgust which he had kept so rigidly controlled until now, Gawain went to him and took him by the shoulders.

"Kay, don't," he said. "Dear friend, don't tear yourself apart. Where should the Grail come, but where it is needed?"

Kay raised his head and looked at him, already fighting his way back to calm, unable even now, even with Gawain, to be at ease in self-revelation.

Shaking a little, he touched Gawain's hands lightly. "At least you're home," he said. He gave a long sigh. "Come – we'll be late for the council."

Until he sat in council, Gawain had not fully understood what was worrying Kay. The Table itself was like a golden lake, gathering to itself all the light of that austere room, diapered with a deeper gold where the names of the knights were displayed. Around it, they sat and wrangled. Gawain remembered the early days, the shining certainties of building Arthur's kingdom. No certainty now, only an unspoken guilt at the kingdom's heart.

Gawain's brother, Sir Agravaine, had launched into a diatribe about some imagined slight to his status, interspersed with spurts of quicksilver malice from Mordred. A few places further round the Table, Gareth was managing to look both bored and miserable. Lancelot was closed in on himself; he might have been praying. The king could well have been asleep; though Gawain knew that his indolent appearance had always concealed a piercingly alert mind, he was suddenly aware of how old Arthur was looking, and tired.

As Gawain examined, anxiously, the face of his king, he saw a shadow fall over it. The room grew dark, as if something had blotted out the sun. An uneasy murmur of voices rose only to die away as, from one of the windows, came a single shaft of light. Light so brilliant, so pure, that Gawain was surprised his eyes could bear it. It cut the shadows and struck the Table like a sword. Gawain saw his own awe and wonder reflected in the faces of his friends.

As they gazed, the Grail came, riding the shaft of light, and hung poised above the Table. A chalice covered with white samite; from it poured the same pure, perpetual light. Gawain felt that he could drink light like water, could bathe in it and wash away all taint. He turned to Kay and saw him young and ardent and adoring, Kay as he should have been, all bitterness leached away.

Gawain did not know how long it was before the incandescence faded, leaving them in the ordinary light of day, the subdued shimmer of the Table. In the silence that still surrounded him, he seemed to hear the voice of an imperative will.

He rose to his feet. "We have seen a great marvel," he said, "and yet the Grail was hidden from us. I swear that I will go from here, and search, and not return until I see the Grail uncovered."

At once, as he had expected, the others were on their feet, repeating the same vow. In the clamour, only two were silent: the king, openly appalled, and Kay, seated with bowed head, his gaze fixed on his clasped hands.

The noise died at last, as the knights left, swept away on the wind of a new venture. Gawain waited until he and Arthur were alone, except for Kay, who had not moved.

"Gawain, you don't know what you've done," Arthur said. He rose and went to the window and spoke to the gathering night. "They won't come back. We'll never sit here together again."

Gawain watched him, but dared not move closer. "Would you have it said that we were granted this vision and did nothing?"

Arthur shrugged. Abruptly he swung round on Kay. "And you?" he asked. "I didn't hear you pledge yourself."

Kay looked up at him, dark eyes unreadable. "I have duties here, my lord."

"Yes, Kay." The king's voice was savage, goaded. "Too often you've put duty before honour."

Kay flinched, but said nothing. Arthur stood staring at him, his breathing ragged, and then stormed off, through the door and up the stair that led to his private rooms.

When the sound of his footsteps had died away, Kay rose at last and came to stand beside Gawain.

"Arthur was wrong," he stated calmly. "You knew exactly what you were doing."

Gawain nodded, half smiling, though he could just as easily have wept. "Isn't it what you wanted?" he asked. "A new direction? Perhaps a new birth? At worst, something worth dying for."

Kay managed to return his smile, infinitely regretful. "I shall miss you, Gawain."

He reached out, tentatively, still finding it hard, as he always had, to release himself, to come out from behind the competent and harsh exterior. Gawain, divining his need, put arms round him and held him.

"Kay, won't you ride with me?" he his asked. "Just for a little while? Arthur would give you leave."

Kay drew back, half reluctant, shaking his head. "I have my duties," he said. "I chose my way long ago; it's too late to turn aside from it now. No, Gawain, you'll ride tomorrow, you and the others, and find adventure, and danger, and perhaps at last you will see the Grail uncovered. And you will return – some of you – bright with honour, and I shall have no share in it. But while you are away, I shall have one inestimable advantage." He paused; his mouth quivered. "I shall be here."

He turned towards the door and the flight of stairs beyond, where the king had withdrawn. Gawain wondered if he had any idea how much of himself he was revealing in that look of patient hunger, the look of a man whose life has had only one real centre.

A stir of movement broke the quiet as a page came down the stairs and into the room. "Sir Kay," he said, "the king calls for you." Something kindled in Kay's eyes; Gawain caught an echo of that ardent look he had seen in the light of the Grail. There was a spot of colour in Kay's face, and he seemed confused, as if he guessed what Gawain was thinking.

"I'll see you again before you go?" he asked.

"Yes, of course."

Briefly Kay clasped Gawain's hand, and then swung round, imperious, as if in that single movement he had put on the High Seneschal's robes. All collected purpose, he left.

Gawain watched him out of sight, and then moved round the golden ellipse of the Table until he came to the window. He saw again the untidy huddle of rooftops that he had seen earlier from the battlements. He was closer to it here, close enough to see smoke drifting upwards from hearth fires, to imagine he could hear the sound of hammers or hoofbeats rising from the crooked streets.

"Yet even here," Gawain said softly, "even here might be the Holy City."

In the Forest Perilous

"You can't go back," said Sir Kay. "You can never go back."

He reined in his tired horse and stared down the forest ride ahead of him. Rain dripped from leafless trees. As the daylight died, the overhanging branches seemed to form a tunnel leading down to darkness.

"Back where?" said Sir Gawain, catching him up so their two mounts stood abreast. He tried to force a cheerful note into his voice. "To the hunting lodge?"

Kay let out a disgusted snort. "That too, though it's not what I meant, Gawain, and well you know it. This morning, Arthur rouses us: 'Let us ride into the Forest Perilous, and see what adventure will befall.' But you can't go back. Not to the days when magic lurked under every bush and a knight could scarcely turn round without stepping into enchantment."

He clicked his tongue and urged his black Morial into motion again, trotting gently down the ride until they had King Arthur in sight. Gawain rode at his side, glancing at the fierce hawk's face, and wondering what Kay had on his mind.

"No, Gawain," the seneschal went on after a few moments. "Those days are gone. No white stags, no enchanted fountains, no faerie damsels luring us to destruction, and the only adventure we're likely to see is a night in the open with no fire and no supper." He shook water from his cloak. "I'm too old for this, Gawain."

Gawain laughed. "Maybe you should stay in Camelot, Grandfather, and toast your feet by the fire."

Kay ignored his friend's teasing. "Those days are gone," he repeated. "Since the great Quest ended, magic has fled. And good riddance, if Arthur could only see it. Kingdoms are built on stone and iron, law and good government, not on airy illusion."

Gawain sighed. He knew Kay was right, and yet… "They were great days," he said. "Days the harpers sing of, even now."

"Harpers!" Kay was all disdain. "Unreliable, every last one of them. You can't run a kingdom on a song, Gawain. And when the way back is closed, you need a way forward. We haven't found it yet. Sometimes I think no one is even looking." He hunched his shoulders under a shower of icy drops from the branches above. "Meanwhile, where is this road taking us?"

He had scarcely spoken when the forest ride began to broaden out, and the trees thinned. Arthur was waiting for them up ahead. As they approached, Gawain began to see lights through the trees, and heard faint music of harps and recorders.

At first he thought they had come to the edge of the forest, but instead they emerged into a wide clearing. The forest ride, which had been leading gently downwards became a paved road winding up a low hill to the gates of a castle. Torches flared at the gates, and light showed in the windows.

"What place is this?" Arthur asked as his knights approached. "Kay, do you know?"

Kay shrugged. "No one who pays us taxes."

"Somewhere to shelter for the night," said Gawain.

Arthur paused, and then began to lead the way up the hill. As he followed, Gawain looked at him and tried to see the joyful, golden young man who had established his kingdom so many years ago. There were glimpses of him still, in the noble, leonine head, the kingly bearing, and yet, Gawain thought, Kay was right. Those days were gone.

At the gate, Kay pulled upon the bell rope. Before he could call out to the porter, the gates swung open silently. Arthur led the way into the courtyard.

The music had grown louder, though the musicians remained unseen. Nor were there grooms to take their horses or servants to lead them indoors. As Gawain looked round, wondering, the gates closed of their own will.

He leant over and murmured to Kay, "Magic has fled?"

The seneschal had a look of icy disapproval as he scanned their surroundings. The courtyard walls were hung with the finest silk, and lamps burnt in silver housings. Instead of the cold rain of the forest, the air was warm, and rich with the scents of summer.

"This is a great wonder!" the king said.

There was a gleam in his eyes, a sudden straightening of his body, as if years had fallen away from him and his youthful strength was renewed.

He laughed as he dismounted. "Let us enter, and take the adventure God has sent us!"

Leaving the horses in the courtyard, they climbed the steps and entered the castle beneath a pointed arch where intricately carved doors stood wide open. The passage beyond was bright with more silver lamps. Tapestries covered the walls and the floor was spread with scented rushes and rose petals.

Arthur was looking around him in wonder, while Kay surveyed everything with the sharp disapproval he reserved for scullions who had failed to complete their tasks. His hand was on his sword hilt. Gawain would have felt like smiling, if he had not shared some of his friend's suspicion. This would not be the first time that a fair outside had concealed evil at its heart.

At the end of the passage was another pair of doors, carved with the shapes of fantastic beasts that were painted in fresh and vivid colours. As Arthur set his hands to the doors to push them open,

Gawain fought with the fancy that one of the dragons might turn its head and sear him with its fire. But the carvings were only carvings.

The music grew louder still as the doors opened. Arthur stepped forward into a hall, with long rows of pillars stretching to the dais at the far end. On the dais was a single, gilded chair, and seated in it, a woman.

Gawain halted, and heard his own breath rough in his throat. The woman was Morgan le Fay.

At his side, Kay stifled an exclamation, and Gawain reached out to touch his arm, a warning to keep silence until they learnt what this might mean. He could feel his friend's coiled tension, and feared that he might release it unwisely.

Queen Morgan sat straight-backed, her hands clasped in her lap. She wore a black gown, with no ornaments except for a belt of linked silver rings, with a bunch of keys hanging from it. Her hair, braided around her head, had turned to pure silver since Gawain saw her last. She was smiling.

Arthur took a few paces down the hall, and bowed with his hand on his breast. "Sister, well met," he said. "It is so long since we have seen or heard of you, I feared you were dead."

"That must have been a great fear," said Morgan, although her tone was amiable. "And no doubt you mourned greatly."

"Madam, you gave us little cause to mourn you," Kay said tartly.

"Sir Kay." Morgan rose, and stretched out her hands. "And Sir Gawain. Be welcome, all of you. All that I have is yours. Chambers are prepared where you may wash and put on fresh garments before supper."

"You expected us to be benighted here, madam?" Kay asked. "Or was it you who twisted the paths?"

"Still the old Kay, I see," said Morgan with a glint of amusement.

"A knight without the burden of courtesy to hold him back might say, 'Still the old Morgan'," Kay retorted.

Morgan came lightly down the steps of the dais, gave one hand to Arthur and held out the other to Kay. "Come, sir, I will have your friendship for tonight at least. Believe me, I intend no harm to any of you." She paused; her eyes were clear and guileless. "Those days are long gone."

For Gawain, the next hours passed in a haze of wonder. Morgan conducted them to a chamber where hot water was provided in silver ewers, with silken robes to exchange for their own travel-stained garments. When they were ready she invited them to table, where the unseen musicians played and food was served on golden dishes, finer than the great feasts of Camelot. From beginning to end, no servants appeared, no one but Morgan herself.

When the meal was over, Gawain expected that they would be dismissed to their bedchambers. Instead, Morgan rose from her place at the head of the table, and said, "Brother, if you will come with me, I have something to show you."

Arthur also rose, and took her hand. "Willingly."

"Not alone, my lord," Kay said instantly.

Morgan's eyes glittered at him. "Does it occur to you, my lord Seneschal, that what I have to show my brother might be for his eyes alone?"

"And does it occur to you, madam, that the king goes nowhere unescorted?"

Morgan would have replied, but Arthur raised a hand. "Peace, sister. I have nothing I wish to hide from Kay or Gawain. We will go together."

She shrugged. "As you please."

Taking down one of the lamps that hung in the hall, she led them to a small door at the back of the dais. Beyond it was a narrow passage of bare stone, a world away from the parts of the castle they had seen so far.

A few yards further on, Morgan came to a door, and selected one of the keys at her waist to open it. Inside she raised her lamp and let the light play over the walls.

At first glance, the room was as bare as the passage outside. There was a single shuttered window with a bench beneath it, and a bed frame stripped of its hangings at the other side of the room. Gawain's first thought was that it was a cell, and Morgan had led them there to imprison them.

Then he saw that the walls were panelled with wood, to the height of a man. On each panel was a painting. Morgan held her lamp up so that its rays spilled over the first panel to the right of the door.

"This is where the story begins."

The panel showed a young man, clad in silver mail and a white surcoat. He was kneeling to receive the accolade of knighthood from a king whose height and tawny-gold hair showed him to be Arthur. The knight himself had a pale, austere face and dark hair cropped short.

"Lancelot!" said Gawain.

Without a word, Morgan moved on. The next panel showed the same young knight, this time kneeling before a woman of great beauty, with a wealth of honey-coloured hair. She was bending over to pin a rose to the knight's surcoat.

"The day she took him as her champion," Arthur murmured.

The next painting covered two panels. It showed a great tournament, with the airy towers of Camelot in the background, behind the silken canopy that covered the royal seats. Arthur and Guenevere were there, with noble guests in the robes of kings. The knight, Lancelot, this time in a surcoat of red and gold, had just vanquished his opponent, who wore a blazon that Gawain recognised ruefully as his own eagle. Queen Guenevere held out to him a gold circlet, the prize of the tourney.

The story went on, with scene after scene in which Lancelot took a victory, or received his reward at the hands of the Queen. Then Morgan let the lamplight fall on the last panel.

Again Lancelot and Guenevere, but this time they were naked. They lay together on grass starred with flowers, and the sun shone down on their coupling.

Arthur turned his head aside, as if he had taken the blow on his cheek, instead of a mortal shaft to the heart.

Kay sprang between his king and the painting, as if he could claw back time so that the king should not have seen it.

"What lie is this?" he asked harshly. "What evil made these images?"

"No evil, sir," said Morgan. "Lancelot himself was my… guest here, and whiled away the time by painting his own story on the panels. Who should know better than he whether he painted lies or truth?"

"And why should we believe you?" Kay asked. "You have failed, time after time, to destroy Arthur, and now you strike at him through his Queen. You would not –"

"Peace, Kay." Arthur gripped his foster brother by the shoulders and then released him. "Words will not wipe the paint away."

Gawain thought that he spoke like a man who reads from a book in a language he does not understand, not one who utters the words of his heart. His eyes were stunned. He sank down on the bench under the window, and bowed his head into his hands. All the renewed vigour of the last hours was gone.

Kay faced Morgan. "Leave us, madam."

For the first time her mask of friendliness slipped, and Gawain saw the venom underneath. "You do not command here, sir." Then she had herself in hand again. She dropped a curtsey, hung the lamp on a bracket, and was gone.

Kay stood looking down at Arthur. His face was pinched, and briefly Gawain saw him as he would be when he was old.

Gawain himself felt no sense of shock. He had known for years that Lancelot and Guenevere were lovers. So had Kay, and so had the rest of the court. He had always believed that Arthur had known it too, but had chosen to do nothing while no one spoke of it openly.

It was out in the open now, and Gawain did not know what the king, or any of them, could do.

Kay took a long breath, and drew himself up, his hawk's face set in fierce contempt. "My lord," he said, "you surely don't believe in this witchery? Morgan has always tried to destroy you, and how better do it than by dividing you from your best knight and your Queen?"

Arthur looked up; his eyes were wary. "Witchery?"

"Do you doubt, my lord, this is Morgan's contriving? Do you believe a word she says? Is it likely that Lancelot would paint his own shame?"

The king let out a sigh; Gawain had never heard a man sound more weary. "Do you speak your heart to me, Kay?"

Their eyes locked together. Gawain could see, for all their estrangement over the years, a deep current of communion running between them.

Kay whispered, "Yes, my lord."

Arthur gazed at him for a moment longer, and then turned to Gawain. "Gawain, I would have your counsel in this."

"My lord, I think that Kay is right," Gawain said carefully. "More likely that Morgan should sow mistrust in your heart, than that Lancelot and the Queen should betray you." He gestured towards the painting. "This proves nothing."

"A torch would quickly end it," Kay said.

The king shook his head. "Why burn what has no meaning?" Betrayingly, he added, "Besides, no one in Camelot will ever see it."

"And no need to speak of such foolishness there," Kay said sharply.

Arthur passed his hands over his face as if he was scrubbing filth away. Heavily, he said. "True, no need to speak – no need at all."

He got up and went out, but Gawain saw that he kept his eyes averted from the painted panel as he passed it.

The next morning Gawain's own garments were returned, clean, to his bedchamber, along with hot water to wash and a tray with spiced wine, rolls and fruit. When he was ready he emerged to find the castle deserted until he met with Kay under the archway that led to the courtyard.

The morning was cool and moist, as if the airs of the forest had been allowed to penetrate this enchanted place. The soft music of the night before was silent; from beyond the walls came the rustle of wind in the trees, like the surge of a vast sea.

In the courtyard their horses were waiting, freshly groomed, and beside them King Arthur and Morgan talked together.

Gawain wished Kay good morning; the seneschal grunted a reply. Gawain thought that he looked exhausted, as if he had not slept.

He laid a hand on Kay's arm. "Are you well?"

Kay shrugged. "I've failed Arthur, time and again," he said, "Somehow I lost the way, and it's too late to find it now. But I've never lied to him, until last night."

"Then I shared it," Gawain said.

Kay took a deep breath. "Dear God, is everything tainted? Is there no honour left?" He pulled his cloak around himself as if against bitter cold. "I said that magic has fled, and I was right. Morgan fills her castle with pretty toys, but those paintings are not magic. I wish to God they were. They're cold truth, standing in daylight.

"There's no way back, Gawain, and no way forward that isn't blocked by Lancelot, standing astride the road. He's too powerful. If

Arthur arraigned him for treachery, his kinsmen would stand with him. The quarrel would split the Table. Arthur's kingdom would go down in flames. What can we do but go on living the lie?"

Gawain shook his head, bewildered, having no counsel for his friend's pain, or his own.

"And for how long, Gawain? Have you asked yourself that?" The seneschal's face was furrowed into lines of bitterness. "How long?"

In the courtyard, Arthur gave his hand to Morgan, and escorted her back to the steps where his knights were waiting.

Gawain heard her say, "No, brother, I will not visit you in Camelot. I will never leave here, until my time comes to go to Avalon, and I will see you there." She smiled at him. "It will not be long, brother, I promise you."

The Last Knight of Camelot

Brother Yves tapped at the door. In all his time as a novice, the monastery had never had a guest so old, so holy, or so downright difficult. Or one to whom so many stories clung.

Swallowing nervously, Yves opened the door, and manoeuvred his tray inside. He was a hulking youth, all feet and elbows, with untidy, straw-coloured hair and guileless blue eyes. There was a three-cornered tear in his sleeve, and one sandal strap needed mending.

The room was cool, shaded. The old man lay on the bed, propped up by pillows. He wore a bedgown of unbleached linen; one thin hand fingered a wooden pectoral cross. Deep, dark eyes regarded Yves from the face of a wild hawk.

"Good morning, sir – Father – your grace," Yves stammered.

"'Sir' will be adequate, thank you." The voice was a blade wrapped in velvet. As Yves placed the tray on his knees, he picked up the spoon and poked distastefully through the mess in the bowl. "Dear God, what's this? Bait for fish? Take it away and bring me some water."

Yves carried the tray to the table by the window where there was a jug of water and cups. As he turned, the light behind him, the old man said,

"Boy? Gareth?" The incisive voice faltered. He brushed cobwebs from his eyes. "For a moment, I thought... You remind me of him, just a little. Gareth... I saw him die. In the courtyard, beside the queen's pyre. His blood hissed in the flames. My gentle Gareth."

The dark eyes were hooded. Yves stepped forward, scarcely breathing.

"Then it's true, sir, what they say? You were one of them – King Arthur's knights? Once, long ago?"

The old man's mouth twisted into a smile. "Yes, it's true. You would think it long ago."

Yves' lips were parted in wonder. "Who were you, sir, when you were in the world? Were you – were you Lancelot?"

A spasm shook the old man, terrifying Yves until he realised it was a fit of silent laughter. "Lancelot? Do you know, that's the funniest thing anyone has said to me in years?" Sobering, he added, "I'm not sure Lancelot would have thought so."

He took the cup; Yves watched him as he drank. His rough habit prickled against his skin. He wondered how it would feel to wear mail, and hold a sword instead of beads.

"You've done so much, sir…" he said wistfully.

"I? No." Passion flared up, a harsh rejection fretting the frail body. "I did nothing. Nothing but live too long, and lose too much."

Yves could not respond. Into the silence came the beating of a bell, the imperative summons of the angelus.

"Go," the old man said. "And take that cat-lap with you. Go to your prayers." His eyes closed. "I was the last and the least of them. Don't wreck your peace of mind on me. I was never worthy."

He could feel the sun, glowing hot beyond closed eyelids. Air moved against his face. Beneath his hand he felt cool blades of grass. He could hear birdsong and the murmur of running water.

He opened his eyes. He lay on his back; above his head, meadowsweet creamed against blue sky, and a butterfly flicked gilded wings to and fro. A voice said, "Kay? Kay, are you awake?"

Hope seized him by the throat. He turned his head. Arthur was seated on the grass beside him – not as Kay had last seen him, harried, grey, defeated, bleeding out his life on the field of Camlann;

this was the lithe, tawny lion of his younger days, watching Kay with a look of sleepy amusement in his amber eyes.

Kay knew that he was dreaming. He only wished the dream to continue. He started up, pulling himself to his knees. Reaching for Arthur's hands, he bent his head over them. His tears spilled out.

"Kay, don't weep." Arthur's voice was warm. "All's well now."

"Oh, no, no –" Kay could barely gasp out the words. "I shall wake and lose you…"

He felt Arthur's hand on his head, forcing him to look up. "Kay, don't you understand? The dream is over. This is the truth. Morning has come." His arms went round Kay and held him in a fierce embrace. "Brother, it's been so long."

Kay wanted to go on clinging to him, but Arthur drew back and stood up. He held out a hand. "Come."

Kay reached out, and saw with wonder that his own hand was firm and young again. A young strength was rising within him; it was still not enough to raise him from his knees. "Where, my lord?"

"To Camelot."

"But that – it's over, gone. Long ago."

"No." Arthur was smiling. "This is the true Camelot, that we tried to build and failed. This Camelot will last for ever. Look."

He stood aside, and Kay saw rising from a froth of apple boughs the airy towers of a castle. It was bright with banners, shining, filled with light. Kay turned his face away; it hurt to go on looking.

"I can't," he said. "I never belonged. I was never worthy."

"None of us is worthy," Arthur said gently. "This is given, not earned." He tugged at Kay's hand. "They're waiting for you – Gawain, Gareth, Lancelot – all the others. We're not complete without you. Come with me."

As Kay listened, he understood at last, and his tears were changed to joy. He allowed his king to raise him, and lead him across the meadow, to the open gates of Camelot.

When Yves returned, the sun had moved round, and light was flooding through the window. The old man's eyes were closed, the fierce face peaceful. The thin, beautiful fingers were folded around the pectoral cross. On the back of his hand a butterfly quivered, raising fragile wings. All the room was filled with the scent of meadowsweet.

About the Author

Cherith Baldry was born in Lancaster, UK, and studied at Manchester University and St Anne's College, Oxford. She worked for some years as a teacher, including a spell as lecturer at Fourah Bay College, Sierra Leone. She is now a full-time writer.

Cherith has published a number of children's novels, under her own name and various pseudonyms. She is currently working as part of the Erin Hunter Warriors series of novels about feral cats, aimed at older children and young adults.

She has also published three adult fantasy novels and a quantity of short fiction in different anthologies and magazines.

She has published short mystery fiction, for example in the anthologies edited by Mike Ashley and published by Robinson. She self-published three mystery novels, *Brutal Terminations*, *Dangerous Deceits* and *Darkest Actions*.

Cherith is widowed with two adult children. She lives in Surrey with one of her sons and two cats. Her interests are travel, reading and music, especially early music.

ALSO FROM NEWCON PRESS

New Adventures of a Chinese Time Machine
First solo novel in two decades from multiple award-winning author **Ian Watson**. When the Chinese Time Machine is hijacked from Oxford, Colonel Maggie Mo is perturbed. Will this mean an end to her trips into the past for 'scientific research', accompanied by her tame British Dons Rajit Sharma and David Mason? Only time will tell...

The Book of Gaheris – Kari Sperring
Gaheris of Orkney, one aof the less celebrated knights of Arthur's court, finds himself up to his neck in intrigue, deception, violence, murder, and old secrets. Clouds gather over Camelot, threatening to destroy all that Arthur and Guenever have built, and Gaheris may be all that stands between Arthur's noble kingdom and disaster.

Birdwatching at the End of the World – G.W. Dexter
Think *Lord of the Flies* but with girls... When the world ends, the pupils of Near School for Girls must fend for themselves on an isolated Scottish island with limited resources, no adults, and no prospect of rescue. As the only boy present, Stephen Ballantyne has to be wary of shifting politics and allegiances as the girls find a way to survive in this new and brutal world.

The Wild Hunt – Garry Kilworth
When Gods meddle in the affairs of mortals, it never ends well... for the mortals, at any rate. Steeped in ancient law, history and imagination, Garry Kilworth serves up an epic Anglo-Saxon saga of swordplay, witches, giants, dwarfs, elves and more, as a young warrior wrongly accused of patricide sets out to clear his name and regain his birthright.

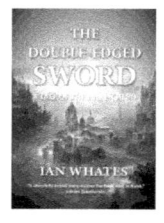

The Double-Edged Sword – Ian Whates
A disgraced swordsman leaves town one step ahead of justice. His past, however, soon catches up with him in the form of Julia, a notorious thief and sometimes assassin. Thrust into an impossible situation, he embarks on what will surely prove to be a suicide mission. "A cheerfully brutal story of betrayal and skulduggery, vicious fun." – *Adrian Tchaikovsky*

www.ingramcontent.com/pod-product-compliance
Ingram Content Group UK Ltd.
Pitfield, Milton Keynes, MK11 3LW, UK
UKHW041813010525
458102UK00002B/75